DESTINY'S
☙TRIUMPHS☙

BOOK 1
IN THE
DESTINY TRILOGY

D.J. PARRISH

ISBN 978-1-64471-022-7 (Paperback)
ISBN 978-1-64471-023-4 (Digital)

Covenant Books, Inc.
11661 Hwy 707
Murrells Inlet, SC 29576
www.covenantbooks.com

In loving memory of my mother, Josephine Russell.
I love you, Mom, with all my heart!

ACKNOWLEDGMENTS

I would like to take this opportunity to acknowledge the following people for their love, support, and contributions while writing this book. I wouldn't have been able to make this dream a reality without you.

I thank God for his guidance and his blessings enabling me to write this book.

I would like to thank my son Kenyatta Parrish for his love and support, allowing me the time to write without any interruptions. I love you!

I would also like to thank my publishing coordinator, Diane Murray, for all her hard work and dedication, helping to make my dream a reality.

David Fall, thank you for being my friend and for dedicating countless late hours reading each chapter, editing my mistakes, and supporting me throughout this venture. I have enjoyed having you on this journey with me.

Teresa Franklin, I thank you for being my friend. You were an inspiration to me, reading, editing, and providing constructive criticism. Thanks for taking this journey with me.

Wardell Dye, thank you for being my friend and reading my work even when you already had a busy schedule. Thank you for believing in me!

Love you all,
D.J.

CHAPTER 1

Reflections

We each have a story to tell, and each story is unique in its own way. This story is unique because it tells of a young African-American girl, Destiny Drake, growing up in a rural area during the twentieth century. The twentieth century was a very unique and stressful time for African-Americans, because it was a time of radical transformations in both the legal and political arenas concerning the status of African-Americans. As a matter of fact, some economic and demographic characteristics of African-Americans weren't too different from the indignities and insolence that they had suffered in the mid-1800s.

By the year 1985, it was time for yet another change! Even though African-Americans were afforded more opportunities, there was still some degree of prejudice that existed in our society, especially in the south and in rural areas.

Destiny was a very beautiful, African-American young lady, twenty-four years of age, with brown eyes and a smile that warmed the heart of everyone she met. Destiny had curly shoulder-length hair with golden hues. The year was 1985, and Destiny had dreams and aspirations of changing the idealism that African-American women could not be independent, smart, beautiful, and successful.

In June of 1985, Destiny left home on the wings of a prayer and the blessings of her family. Destiny carried in her possession a tattered brown suitcase, which contained her best jeans, six shirts, two dresses, a pair of dress shoes, two pairs of sneakers, a picture of her with her family, a Bible, a set of pearls given to her by her aunt, and three hundred dollars.

Destiny was excited because she was determined to change how society viewed African-American women; she had joined the Army and was prepared to fight for her rights and the rights of others who were not able to fight for themselves and to be a voice for African-Americans everywhere. She would make a positive difference in the fight for freedom and justice. Destiny didn't know it, but she was in for a very rude awakening, for the change she hoped to formulate would be slow to reach fruition.

Destiny had been assigned to Fort Jackson, South Carolina, to complete her basic training instructions. South Carolina didn't have the homey feel that she was used to. The people there were rude, unfriendly, and, to a certain degree, somewhat prejudice. It was June 15, 1985. Destiny had completed her battery of tests and passed the required physical, and she was ready to proceed to her training station. Destiny was given a one-way plane ticket from her home state, Arkansas, to South Carolina.

Destiny arrived at the airport in South Carolina. She was tired, hungry, and in desperate need of a nap. She was met by a boy who appeared to be no older than seventeen, dressed in a green military uniform with combat boots, holding a sign with her name on it. Destiny approached the young soldier and presented him with the paperwork she had received upon completing her physical and testing. The soldier took the documentation and Destiny's bag and led her to a green sedan with a decal on the door that read "United States Army." The young man opened the door for Destiny and stored her suitcase in the trunk of the car.

The soldier said, "I am sorry for not introducing myself when you first walked over, but my name is Specialist (SPC) Jerome Bryce. I work at the post that you are assigned to, and since I am the duty driver today, it is my responsibility to ensure you arrive at the unit safely."

Destiny replied, "Thank you for picking me up, and it is nice to meet you, SPC Bryce."

The remainder of the trip was ridden in silence, because Destiny was exhausted and SPC Bryce had to pay attention to the traffic.

An hour later, Destiny and SPC Bryce arrived at the 4th Basic Combat Training Brigade. SPC Bryce informed Destiny, "Destiny, you will be assigned to Echo Company, 14th Battalion, according to your orders. Someone from that unit will pick you up tomorrow." Destiny waited until SPC Bryce unlocked the trunk and retrieved her suitcase, handing it to her. SPC Bryce said, "Please report to the front desk and sign in with the charge of quarters (CQ) Staff Sergeant (SSG) Buckley. He will assign you a room for the night." Destiny nodded and did as she was told.

Destiny was assigned a room in the female barracks on the first floor. The room was small in comparison to the rooms Destiny was accustomed to seeing back home. The walls were a dreary white color, and the room was musty and stuffy, as if no one had used it in quite some time. There was a community shower and a bathroom down the hall from the room Destiny was assigned to. SPC Bryce escorted her to the room and then walked her to the dining facility (mess hall) for dinner (chow). SPC Bryce sat and ate supper with Destiny in the dining facility. Both Destiny and SPC Bryce had baked chicken, rice with brown gravy, green beans, corn bread, iced tea, and cherry Jell-O. Once they had finished their dinner, SPC Bryce walked Destiny back to her building and said, "Good night, Destiny. I will wake you up in the morning." Destiny nodded okay and went into her room. Destiny showered and went straight to sleep.

It was still dark outside, four o'clock (0400), when SPC Bryce woke Destiny. SPC Bryce said, "You have thirty minutes to get dressed, and then I will return to walk you to breakfast!" Destiny dressed in a pair of jeans, a red button-down blouse, and red sneakers and put her hair up in a bun. She had five minutes to spare before SPC Bryce knocked on her door again.

SPC Bryce inquired, "Did you sleep well last night?"

Destiny replied, "I slept very well. Thanks for asking."

It was four forty (0440) when Destiny and SPC Bryce finished eating. SPC Bryce informed Destiny that she should repack her suitcase and report to the CQ desk with her suitcase and room key. SSG

Tyson called SPC Bryce and informed him that someone from Echo Company would be there to pick Destiny up at five fifteen (0515).

At precisely five fifteen (0515), a green truck-type vehicle with rails on the back pulled up in front of the CQ office. A female wearing a big brown hat (her hat resembled the one that Smokey Bear wears), shiny combat boots, and a camouflage uniform entered the CQ office and inquired about Private First Class (PFC) Destiny Drake. Destiny stood, her back ramrod straight and her face emotionless, and stated with confidence, "Ma'am, I am PFC Destiny Drake!" The female Drill Sergeant (Staff Sergeant) Tyson was impressed with Destiny's manners. Drill Sergeant Tyson said, "PFC Drake, secure your bags and please go sit in the passenger seat of the vehicle." PFC Destiny Drake did as she had been told. Drill Sergeant Tyson thanked SPC Bryce for picking up Destiny and providing her with a room upon her arrival. SPC Bryce said, "Drill Sergeant Tyson, you are most welcome." Drill Sergeant Tyson entered the truck and left.

Drill Sergeant Tyson explained, "It is a two-hour ride to Echo Company. You will be assigned to 4th Platoon, and your drill sergeants will be Drill Sergeant Ross and Drill Sergeant Seanne, both males." Drill Sergeant Tyson noticed that PFC Drake had long fingernails and nice curly hair and was wearing minimal makeup. Drill Sergeant Tyson was positive that her counterparts, Drill Sergeants Ross and Seanne, would consider PFC Drake as being "prissy," due to her appearance.

Two hours later, Drill Sergeant Tyson and PFC Drake arrived at their destination, Echo Company. Destiny saw this big hulk of a guy, who appeared to stand seven feet tall. His shoulders were broad and looked like boulders; his uniform looked as if it was molded onto his body. His arms resembled large tree trunks, but his waist was tiny for a man his size. Around his waist was a green military belt that accented its smallness. Even in uniform, Destiny could see the bulging muscles that this man had for legs. According to the name on his uniform, this was Seanne. As soon as the truck stopped, this "hulk" of an individual, Drill Sergeant Seanne, walked over to the vehicle, grabbed the passenger door, snatched it open, and yelled at Destiny, "Get out of the truck! Get your bag and fall in over with the other soldiers!" Destiny continued to sit in the truck and wait for Drill Sergeant Seanne to finish his tirade and move away from the truck, so that she might exit the vehicle when this hulk of a man asked her nicely.

Drill Sergeant Seanne took one look at Destiny's stern face and thought that Destiny was failing to obey his instruction, so he stepped back and said, "Would you like a personal invitation to exit the vehicle, private?"

Destiny looked Drill Sergeant Seanne right in his eyes and stated, "It would be nice if you asked me politely, sir!" Drill Sergeant Seanne threw his head back and gave a hearty belly laugh.

Drill Sergeant Seanne had already come to the conclusion that Destiny was "prissy" by the way she dressed and the fact that she had long nails that were painted the color of her outfit, but now, he had also concluded that she was a "smart-mouthed troublemaker" as well. Drill Sergeant Seanne called to his counterpart, Drill Sergeant Ross, "We have a prima donna over here. We got our work cut out for us. This new soldier is a prima donna!"

Drill Sergeant Ross was the opposite of Drill Sergeant Seanne. Drill Sergeant Ross was about five feet and eight inches, with broad shoulders with smooth muscles. Drill Sergeant Ross was African-American; he had black curly hair, a complexion the color of toasted caramel, thick legs with bulging muscles, and a tiny waist. Drill Sergeant Ross also had dimples that accented his smile; he was what most women would consider a "pretty boy."

Drill Sergeant Ross told Drill Sergeant Seanne, "Seanne, leave the soldier alone. Allow me to help PFC Drake adjust." Drill Sergeant Ross walked to the truck and said these words to Destiny, "PFC Drake, would you please get out of the truck and join us over in the training area?"

Destiny said in her most polite voice, "Thank you, sir. I would be honored to join you all for training; at least one of you has some manners."

Destiny had no idea that Drill Sergeant Ross was being sarcastic. She sat and waited for Drill Sergeant Ross to be polite and give her a hand getting out of the vehicle, but that didn't happen. Destiny suddenly felt hands around her waist lifting her slight frame from the vehicle and sitting her unceremoniously on her bottom at the back of the formation. Destiny was furious. She jumped up off the ground, eyes blazing and hands on her hips, and stated, "How dare you, you big oaf, put your hand on my person! If you even think of coming near me again, I will sock you in the eye!" Drill Sergeant Seanne walked over to Destiny and picked her up by the scruff of her shirt, her feet dangling in the air, and she was face-to-face with Drill Sergeant Seanne. Drill Sergeant Seanne said, "This is how I handle prima donnas who think they are in charge! Now when I put you down, I expect you to get your bag and fall in line with the other soldiers. Am I clear, private?" Destiny did not answer Drill Sergeant Seanne; instead, she hung from the tips of his fingers and gave him a glaring look that would have made lesser men quiver in their boots. Drill Sergeant Seanne lowered Destiny gently from her position, placing her upon her feet in front of him. Destiny was so angry she wanted to kick the big oaf in his shins, yet she refrained. He made her so *mad* she was seeing red! Drill Sergeant Seanne could see the unshed tears that Destiny refused to release, and he realized there was more to this waif of a woman than one could imagine.

Destiny squared her shoulders, picked up her suitcase, and walked with her head held high behind the last female in line. Drill Sergeant Seanne walked beside Destiny, and he was impressed to see that Destiny was able to keep in step as he sang cadence, not missing a beat; he wasn't sure if this was due to her anger or her actual ability to march.

The group marched for what appeared to be a mile to Destiny. Destiny's bun had wisps of hair hanging down that had escaped during her march, and there was sheen of sweat covering her face.

Drill Sergeant Seanne walked up to Destiny and said, "Private, I see you were able to keep up during the march, unlike some of your counterparts who fell behind. Have you been practicing for your training here?" Destiny ignored Drill Sergeant Seanne. Destiny was still livid with Drill Sergeant Seanne for his being able to extract a laugh from the other soldiers at her expense. Drill Sergeant Seanne looked at Destiny and stated, "Not only are you a troublemaker, but you are hard of hearing too!"

Destiny could not contain her anger any longer; she stepped in front of Drill Sergeant Seanne, put her hands on her hips, rolled her head from side to side, and asked, "What did I do to you to make you hate me so much? I will prove to you that I am capable of handling myself and any punishment that you can dish out!"

Drill Sergeant Seanne smiled at Destiny and said, "You cannot imagine the amount of punishment I can inflict upon you."

Destiny looked at Drill Sergeant Seanne and told him, "Take your best shot. I am sure I have dealt with worst people than the likes of you!"

Drill Sergeant Ross screamed, "*Halt!*" The group stopped, and Drill Sergeant Ross said, "*Take a seat!*" The entire group with the exception of Destiny looked totally exhausted, ready to fall down. Drill Sergeant Ross walked to the back of the line where Destiny was located and asked, "PFC Drake, how are you doing?"

Destiny replied, "I am fine. Why are we stopping?"

Drill Sergeant Ross explained, "I thought the group could use a break. Would you like some water?"

Destiny replied, "No, thank you, but may I move to the front of the line away from this big oaf?"

Drill Sergeant Ross began to smile and stated, "How about Drill Sergeant Seanne and I trade places for a while?" Drill Sergeant Ross then asked Destiny, "PFC Drake, according to your paperwork, you have some past training in the Reserve Officers' Training Corps (ROTC). Would you mind calling cadence for the group?"

Destiny looked at Drill Sergeant Ross and stated, "Yes, I participated in the corps training while at the university that I attended, and I would love to call cadence (sing military songs to motivate the group and keep them in step)." This would be an opportunity for Drill Sergeant Ross to see if PFC Drake had a voice to match the temper she had shown earlier.

Drill Sergeant Ross informed Drill Sergeant Seanne, "I am moving PFC Drake to the front of the group with me, so that she can call cadence."

Drill Sergeant Seanne laughed and stated, "I doubt that prima donna could sing her way out of a cracker box!"

Drill Sergeant Ross stated, "Lighten up on PFC Drake and give her a chance, Seanne."

Fifteen minutes later, Drill Sergeant Ross called, "*On your feet! Fall in!*" Then Drill Sergeant Ross called PFC Drake out of the group beside him, and he asked her, "Do you know any marching cadences?" Destiny nodded her head and looked at Drill Sergeant Ross; he nodded for her to proceed with the cadence. Destiny opened her mouth and uttered these words in a clear and strong voice that could be heard for a quarter of a mile:

*I don't know why I left
But I know I must've done wrong
And it won't be long
'Till I get on back home*

*Got a letter in the mail
Go to war or go to jail
Sat me in that barber's chair
Spun me around, I had no hair;*

*Used to drive a Cadillac
Now I pack it on my back
Used to drive a limousine
Now I'm wearing Army green*

*Dress it right and cover down
Forty inches all around
Nine to the front and six to the rear
That's the way we do it here*

*Used to date a beauty king
Now I date my M16
Ain't no use in lookin' down
Ain't no discharge on the ground*

Ain't no use in looking back
Jody's got your Cadillac
Ain't no use in calling home
Jody's got your girl and gone

Ain't no use in feeling blue
Jody's got your sister too
Took away my faded jeans
Now I'm wearing Army green

They took away my gin and rum
Now I'm up before the sun

Mama, Mama, can't you see
What this Army's done to me?
Mama, Mama, can't you see
This Army life is killing me.

Drill Sergeant Seanne was so shocked. He ran from the back of the group to the front of the group to see who was singing. Drill Sergeant Seanne asked Drill Sergeant Ross, "Was that the prima donna singing?"

Drill Sergeant Ross stated, "That was PFC Drake singing that cadence, Drill Sergeant Seanne."

Drill Sergeant Seanne just nodded his head and jogged back to the rear of the group. Drill Sergeant Seanne thought, *Maybe there is more to this waif of a woman than meets the eye. I cannot believe she sang that cadence that damn good, not to mention she had a damn good singing voice too!*

Finally, the group had reached their destination: the issue point. The soldiers would be fitted for uniforms, boots, physical training (PT) gear, and other military gear that they would need, to include a duffle bag to carry everything in.

Drill Sergeant Seanne walked to the front of the line, and he said these words to PFC Drake, "PFC Drake, you did a very good job singing that cadence."

PFC Drake responded, "Thank you, Drill Sergeant Seanne!"

Drill Sergeant Ross shook his head and smiled, because at that moment, he realized two things: First, PFC Drake was a fighter, and she was full of surprises. Second, Drill Sergeant Seanne would have a very hard time breaking PFC Drake's spirit.

PFC Drake, PFC Turner, PFC Thornton, PFC Carter, and PFC Falls were all called to the front of the line to receive their gear first, due to their rank. That was when Destiny realized that rank had its privileges. Destiny was senior to the other soldiers who were called, so she put her gear in her duffle bag and helped the other female soldiers put their gear together and get it in order and secure it in their duffle bag as well.

Drill Sergeant Ross nudged Drill Sergeant Seanne upon witnessing PFC Drake taking on the role as a leader with her peers.

PFC Carter, an overweight Caucasian girl, about five feet and five inches tall, who had crooked teeth that were stained brown from chewing tobacco and had a slight limp when she walked, asked Destiny, "Where did you learn to sing like that? You got a pretty voice."

Destiny said, "Thank you, PFC Carter." Destiny also said, "PFC Carter, where are you from?"

PFC Carter stated, "I am from Alabama."

Destiny told her, "I guess it would be safe to say we are neighbors, because I am from Arkansas."

PFC Thornton stated, "I am from Arkansas too."

PFC Drake asked, "What city are you from?"

PFC Thornton stated, "I am from Little Rock, Arkansas."

Drill Sergeant Seanne interrupted their conversation speaking these words, "PFC Drake, I need you to call cadence on the way back to garrison."

PFC Drake looked at Drill Sergeant Seanne and said, "Yes, sir, Drill Sergeant Seanne." Destiny's response took Drill Sergeant Seanne by surprise; he was expecting Destiny to refuse, so that he could order her to do pushups.

Weeks and months began to go by, and PFC Drake continued to improve and show that she was a leader. During week 4 of training, PFC Carter was having trouble keeping up with the group during the morning run while doing PT. PFC Drake had completed the run, but she ran all the way back to where PFC Carter was struggling to put one foot in front of the other. PFC Drake spoke these words to PFC Carter, "I will not leave you, but you must continue to run. I will sing cadence so that you can remain focused and run. Please stay with me." Drill Sergeant Seanne could not believe what he was seeing; the prima donna was truly concerned about her fellow soldiers.

Both PFC Carter and PFC Drake ran to the barracks, took their showers, and dressed for the day.

Drill Sergeant Ross saw PFC Drake when she exited the barracks, and he walked over and told her, "PFC Drake, how would you like to work with PFC Carter during PT?"

PFC Drake said, "I would be happy to work with her, Drill Sergeant Ross."

Despite the extra time that PFC Drake spent working with PFC Carter, she was not able to pass her PT test the first time.

PFC Drake asked Drill Sergeant Ross, "Drill Sergeant, do you think it would help PFC Carter if I ran the test with her?"

Drill Sergeant Ross told PFC Drake, "I will allow you to run with her. As a matter of fact, I will allow you to take the test with her!"

Three days later, both Drill Sergeant Ross and Drill Sergeant Taylor administered the PT test to PFC Carter, and PFC Drake did the test alongside her. PFC Carter was able to perform sixty-three pushups and seventy-two sit-ups and ran the two miles in fourteen minutes and twenty seconds. PFC Carter was so surprised when Drill Sergeant Taylor announced, "PFC Carter, congratulations, you have just passed your PT test." PFC Carter began to cry, and she hugged PFC Drake, thanking her for the help. For the first time in a long time, PFC Drake had a sense of belonging and doing the right thing.

Time had flown by, PFC Drake and the rest of the Fourth Platoon had passed their PT test, and they had to qualify with their individual weapon at the range and perform the ten-mile march in order to graduate. PFC Drake was proud of herself; she had accomplished all her tasks up to this point. PFC Drake felt that Drill Sergeant Seanne was no longer referring to her as "the prima donna," but instead he referred to her as "PFC Drake," saying her name with respect instead of as if he loathed her.

Drill Sergeant Seanne and Drill Sergeant Ross worked day and night with their soldiers, training and retraining, ensuring these soldiers were ready for the range and the final march. The day finally arrived; the platoon went to the range. Everyone had qualified with the exception of PFC Drake and PFC Carter. PFC Carter finally qualified using her M16 weapon.

PFC Carter asked Drill Sergeant Seanne, "May I coach PFC Drake so that she may qualify?"

Drill Sergeant Seanne said, "Go ahead. This soldier could not hit the broad side of the barn, so it can't hurt."

PFC Drake was becoming more frustrated by the minute, and she knew she must qualify to graduate basic training. All she could think of was, *I refuse to spend another day on this range in the presence of Drill Sergeant Seanne, because if I do, I fear I will shoot the man!* PFC Carter jumped down in the fox hole beside PFC Drake. PFC Carter said, "PFC Drake, I want you to imagine that Drill Sergeant Seanne is the target, and I expect you to shoot him!" PFC Drake was upset at Drill Sergeant Seanne because of his comment about her not being able to shoot a barn. PFC Drake took aim, imagined her target being Drill Sergeant Seanne, and scored forty-eight rounds, which was almost a perfect score. There were only fifty rounds total to earn a perfect score.

Drill Sergeant Seanne asked PFC Drake, "How did you manage to shoot an almost perfect score?"

PFC Drake stated, "I just imagined you were the target!"

Drill Sergeant Seanne and Drill Sergeant Ross both guffawed at PFC Drake's answer.

Three days later, the entire platoon made the ten-mile road march. The soldiers had bonded over the three months that they had been together. One might even consider them a family! The time had come for each soldier to begin thinking about how life would be without their fellow soldiers. Drill Sergeant Ross and Drill Sergeant

Seanne informed the soldiers, "You all will be receiving your orders tomorrow. Some of you may be stationed at the same duty stations, while others of you will be stationed at other places." The morning had arrived; the platoon was excited to see who was going where. Drill Sergeant Seanne called off the following personnel: "PFC Drake, PFC Carter, Private Christian, Private Banks, please report to me!" PFC Carter, Private Christian, and Private Banks all received orders going to Fort Sam Houston. PFC Drake received orders to Fort Gordon, Georgia. PFC Drake was so disappointed that she would not be seeing her new friend PFC Carter.

PFC Drake graduated from her basic training class with honors, which surprised her tremendously. After graduation, PFC Drake introduced Drill Sergeant Seanne to her mother, Althea. Drill Sergeant Seanne told PFC Drake's mother these words, "Ma'am, when I first met your daughter, I was sure she would not make it through this training. She was the smallest person here, but I found she had the biggest heart. PFC Drake has a fighter spirit, and she will do well wherever she goes. I am proud to say you did an extraordinary job in rearing a fine young lady." PFC Drake began to wipe away a tear, for she thought Drill Sergeant Seanne hated her.

Drill Sergeant Seanne asked to speak to PFC Drake alone, and he told her, "PFC Drake, I misjudged you. When I met you, I thought you were 'prissy, a prima donna.' PFC Drake, I am proud of the soldier that you have become, and I would be happy to serve with you in the future."

PFC Drake wiped tears from her eyes twice in one day, tears that were present due to the nice things Drill Sergeant Seanne said to and about her. PFC Drake left Fort Jackson, South Carolina, that evening with her head held high and with new knowledge. PFC Drake had learned a very valuable lesson while training under the tutelage of Drill Sergeant Seanne. First, PFC Drake learned that appearances can be deceiving. People are not always as they appear to be; size does not determine the character or the heart of an individual. Second, PFC Drake learned that she reminded Drill Sergeant Seanne of someone he had once cared for deeply, and he had lost that individual to drugs before he came in the military. Finally, PFC Drake learned that when someone sees potential in you, that individual will push you beyond your limits to ensure you reach your full potential or the goals that have been set forth for you.

CHAPTER 2

Duty

Part 1

P FC Destiny Drake had been busy these past six months, and her accomplishments were tremendous, since leaving Arkansas in June of 1985. Destiny successfully attended and graduated from the United States Army's Basic Training Boot Camp as well as the Army's Advanced Individual Training (AIT) required for her Military Occupational Specialty (MOS) 74C—Telecommunications Operator and Maintainer.

PFC Drake received permanent change of station (PCS) orders to Korea, her first permanent duty station, assigned to the 1st Signal Brigade. Destiny was happy to be able to work a job utilizing her newly learned skills, yet she was sad, because she would not be able to visit her family for an entire year. Destiny wondered, *What will Mama think when I don't come home for a year? I hope she won't think that I have abandoned the family!*

Destiny worked directly for the Brigade Commander, Colonel Thornton. Destiny was responsible for ensuring that Colonel Thornton was able to communicate at all times, when in his office as well as when traveling in his vehicle to other locations within the country. Destiny had a very important job, because she was responsible for ensuring that the colonel's secure telephone would work and his classified internet connections for his computer up and run-

ning so that he might send and receive messages without any hic-
cups and she must make sure his secure communication keys were
always up-to-date so that he would be able to get online and have
conferences and teleconferences at a minute's notice. In order for
Destiny to be available to perform these duties, Colonel Thornton
had requested that PFC Drake be his driver and technical assistant.
Destiny was also responsible for preparing any and all emails, letter
correspondence, and maintaining Colonel Thornton's itinerary and
calendar. Destiny was proficient in all her duties and maintained the
security requirements by ensuring there was no breach of classified or
confidential information at any time.

It had been six months since Destiny had been working for
Colonel Thornton, and yet Colonel Thornton still had difficulty
remembering her name, so he referred to Destiny simply as "PFC."
Destiny would respond diligently when Colonel Thornton addressed
her as such and continued to perform all her duties in an exemplary
manner, yet Destiny was a little annoyed that he could not remember
her name after six months. Despite his lack of remembering Destiny's
name, Colonel Thornton was very impressed with Destiny's perfor-
mance and would often brag about Destiny to other officers during
meetings by saying, "My PFC has more knowledge concerning the
military operations and is more proficient at communicating than
most of you! Some of you could consider her the example which you
should follow when conducting yourself." This would anger most of
the officers, for they did not like being compared to a very young,
female, African-American soldier, especially a Private First Class. The
one individual that this infuriated the most was Second Lieutenant
(2LT) Cedric James. Each time 2LT James would enter the brigade
for any training, he made it a point to intimidate and disrespect PFC
Drake, not to mention his belittling her in front of his fellow officers.
Destiny would hate to see 2LT James enter the brigade, for she knew
it was just a matter of time before she became his target. Destiny
would ignore his taunts as best she could, but she wished she could
tell him to go to hell. Destiny was a praying woman, and she knew
God heard her prayers. It was just a matter of time before 2LT James
would get what he deserved.

One day, 2LT James entered Destiny's office, wanting to schedule an appointment to see Colonel Thornton. PFC Drake had just received her promotion to SPC Drake and was preparing the notes for Colonel Thornton's morning brief, when 2LT James walked over to Destiny's desk. 2LT James called to SPC Drake and said, "Private Drake, get me a cup of coffee." SPC Drake rose from her seat, closing the laptop that contained the brief that she was typing, and walked to the table with the coffee and doughnuts.

SPC Drake poured a cup of coffee and placed a doughnut on a napkin and asked, "Sir, would you like sugar and cream in your coffee? If so, how much sugar would you prefer?"

2LT James glared at Destiny, and he spoke the following words, "No, private, I want my coffee black like you!"

Destiny stood and counted to ten silently, before turning to face 2LT James. Her first instinct was to throw the hot coffee in his face, but she refrained. Colonel Thornton watched from his office's door. Destiny lifted the cup of black coffee along with the napkin containing the doughnut and carried it to 2LT James. James was sitting on the couch.

Destiny waited until 2LT James rose from the couch before she presented him with the coffee and doughnut, which was considered proper etiquette. 2LT James stood and took the items from Destiny, ensuring that he spilled some of the sweltering hot coffee on her hand. Destiny flinched but made no sound despite her first instinct being her wanting to punch that fool in his throat; but she refrained, as 2LT James had hoped she would. Colonel Thornton walked from his position near the door and said, "SPC Drake, I think you should go to the infirmary and tell the medic to check your hand and report back to me with the results!" 2LT James was staggered to hear Colonel Thornton speak. That meant he could have witnessed the entire ordeal. SPC Drake said, "Yes, sir!"

To 2LT James, Colonel Thornton walked over and stood directly in front of the junior officer and said, "If SPC Drake has sustained a burn on her hand due to your mistreatment of her, I will have your ass! You will first apologize to SPC Drake upon her return. Second, you will address her as SPC Drake, since she was promoted earlier this week. And, third, you will be placed on duty for the next ninety days. You will also forfeit one-half of your pay for three months, and you will then be reassigned to another duty station! SPC Drake will not be disrespected by you or any other person while I am in charge of this brigade, and you will treat her with the same respect as you would treat me! Do I make myself clear, lieutenant?"

2LT James replied sheepishly, "Yes, sir."

A half hour later, SPC Drake returned from the infirmary and knocked on Colonel Thornton's door. Colonel Thornton called, "Enter." SPC Drake entered as she had been told and stood five paces from the desk and centered herself in front of Colonel Thornton's desk and said, "Sir, SPC Drake requests permission to speak." Colonel Thornton nodded.

Destiny said, "Sir, SSG Armstrong, the senior medic at the infirmary, stated that I had sustained a second-degree burn from the coffee."

Colonel Thornton stated, "SPC Drake, please have a seat on the sofa there, and I will be right back."

SPC Drake did as she was told. Five minutes later, Colonel Thornton returned, with 2LT James in tow. SPC Drake stood at the position of attention when Colonel Thornton entered his office. Again, Colonel Thornton told Destiny, "Please have a seat, SPC Drake." Destiny sat on the couch again as she had been told. The colonel motioned for 2LT James to have a seat without looking in his direction.

Colonel Thornton spoke, "SPC Drake, I apologize for the injuries you sustained this morning, and I will assure you, it will never happen again!"

SPC Drake said, "Thank you, sir."

Colonel Thornton then looked at 2LT James for the first time. Colonel Thornton looked at 2LT James as if he was scum, left on the bottom of his boot, and ordered, "Lieutenant James, I believe you have something that you need to tell SPC Drake."

SPC Drake had risen from her seat and stood at parade rest, but 2LT James ordered, "SPC Drake, please have a seat." Then 2LT James said, "I hope you can find it within your heart to please forgive me for my actions this morning. I am not used to young soldiers such as yourself being given so much authority, yet you remained humble through my ill-treatment of you. I was wrong to treat you with such disrespect and malice. Please forgive me for doing so."

SPC Drake stood, and she said, "Sir, I forgive you for the hateful words that you spoke to me earlier today, and I forgive you for being disrespectful; but I will not apologize for the color of my skin, nor will I apologize for the manners that my parents have taught me. Sir, I feel sorry for you because your heart has been hardened with hate and you see a difference instead of embracing the diversity that exists. You create barriers where there should be none." SPC Drake then turned her attention to Colonel Thornton and asked, "Sir, may I please be excused? I have a great deal of work to be completed, and I must ensure your teleconference is scheduled and the equipment is set up for tomorrow."

Colonel Thornton did something that Destiny was not expecting; he stood and said, "SPC Drake, I salute you for having the fortitude to accept the responsibilities that you have been charged with and the courage for being the strong, professional soldier that you are!"

Destiny returned Colonel Thornton's salute, and a tear slid from her eye, for it was at that moment that she knew she had earned his utmost respect.

The following morning, SPC Drake reported to work an hour earlier than normal. She ensured that Colonel Thornton's teleconference was set up, tested the equipment to ensure it was working properly, and placed a vase upon Colonel Thornton's desk with three yellow roses and a card that simply read, "Thank you, sir." Colonel Thornton arrived at the brigade and headed straight to the teleconference. SPC Drake ensured that there was coffee made and clean cups with saucers for every officer seated at the table.

SPC Drake waited until Colonel Thornton was seated, and she poured his coffee and inquired, "Sir, will there be anything else?"

Colonel Thornton said, "Yes, SPC Drake, could you be so kind as to explain the communications part of this brief?"

SPC Drake said, "Yes, sir, I would be honored to explain that portion of your brief."

Colonel Thornton smiled and nodded. SPC Drake explained the details of communication, the required equipment, and how the equipment should be set up for maximum results and answered any questions that were asked. Colonel Thornton was very impressed with the manner in which Destiny explained everything, the patience in answering the most mundane question, and her ability to remain focused at all times, even when addressing the General of the Army, and reassuring him she would be available to maintain all communications for Colonel Thornton. Colonel Thornton finished the teleconference and dismissed the officers who attended.

SPC Drake cleaned the conference room, secured the equipment, turned off the lights, locked the door, and returned to the brigade. As soon as Colonel Thornton heard SPC Drake in the outer office area, he said, "SPC Drake, could you please step into my office?" SPC Drake did as she was told.

Colonel Thornton said, "SPC Drake, please have a seat. I am most impressed with the work that you have been doing while assigned to this brigade. I realized your tour of duty is fast coming to a close, but I would be most appreciative if you could spend one more year working in your present capacity. Oh, by the way, SPC Drake, thank you for the flowers. They were a lovely touch to the office!"

SPC Drake immediately said, "Sir, I would love to spend another year working under your command. Sir, would it be possible for me to take leave at the close of my first year and visit my family?"

Colonel Thornton said, "SPC Drake, absolutely, you can take a month off to visit your family, and I look forward to your returning and continuing the great work that you have been doing!"

Destiny completed her first tour of duty in the 1st Signal Brigade, and she felt a sense of pride in her accomplishments during her tour. Colonel Thornton was true to his word, and he allowed SPC Drake to take one month of leave to go visit her family.

Part 2

On July 3, 1986, Destiny returned to Arkansas after having been gone for over a year. Her entire family met her at the airport in Little Rock, and her mother immediately noticed the changes in her daughter. Her mother observed that her baby girl left home over a year ago, but in her stead, this beautiful woman returned.

Althea Drake was very proud of the woman her daughter, Destiny, had become. Althea was a beautiful woman in her own right. She had smooth skin the color of toasted almonds; her shape was indicative of a woman who had borne children; the girth of her hips was wide without being offensive; she had a beautiful face with minimal wrinkles; and her hair was long, thick, and brown coils that she wore wound into a bun at the nape of her neck. When she smiled, she had beautiful pearly white teeth, with a small gap between the two front teeth, thus providing an air of sexiness. She was a proud woman who stood ramrod straight with her head held high. Althea always chose to see "the best" in others, rather than the worst.

Destiny retrieved her duffle from the luggage conveyor belt, set it on the floor beside her, ran to her mother, and gave her a hug and kissed her on the cheek. Destiny was ecstatic to see her family, especially her mother. Destiny opened her backpack and removed a gift box wrapped in bright-yellow paper with a red ribbon and said, "Mama, I brought you a gift from Korea. I hope you like it." Althea took the gift box and gingerly untied the ribbon, folding it and placing it in her purse; and then she slowly unwrapped the beautiful wrapping paper, making sure not to allow her excitement to tear it, folding it neatly and placing it beside the ribbon. Althea always opened each gift that Destiny gave her in the same meticulous manner, preserving the moment! Then she opened the box. Inside the box was an ivory music box, with intricate carvings on the top and her name inscribed in gold lettering; and when Althea lifted the lid, the song "Beautiful" was twinkling from the box.

Althea hugged Destiny and said, "Thank you, baby. This is so beautiful. I especially like that this music box is playing my favorite song. I will treasure it always."

Destiny said, "You are welcome, Mama. I love you."

The Drake family left the airport and began their journey to Camden.

Three hours later, "the Drakes" arrived home. Destiny noticed the house seemed smaller now than when she left a year ago. As usual, Althea's rose bushes were loaded with fragrant flowers, and Destiny could not resist picking one of the white roses and sniffing it. Destiny said, "I truly missed home and each of you!" Althea went inside and changed into a comfortable house dress and began to prepare a feast for Destiny's return. That night, Althea made all Destiny's favorites: fried chicken, collard greens with ham hocks, corn on the cob, mashed potatoes, corn bread, apple pie, and sweet tea.

Destiny sampled each dish heartily, smiling, and said, "Mama, there is nobody who can cook like you. This is really good!"

Althea smiled and said, "Thank you, baby. I am glad you enjoyed this meal. I truly missed you."

Word spread like wildfire that Destiny was home; and all her cousins, aunts, uncles, nieces, and nephews came over the next day to see her. Since it was the 4th of July, there was a feast waiting to be had! To Destiny's surprise, there was one other person who came to welcome her home: her best friend, Eric Crawford. When Destiny was young, she and Eric were inseparable; most thought that the two would wed. But instead, Eric left Camden and moved to Dallas, Texas, to attend the university; and Destiny joined the Army. So this was the first contact the two had had in over a year.

Eric hugged Destiny and said, "Destiny, you sure look good. It would appear as though you put on a little weight, but it looks great on you." Eric was six feet and two inches tall and had a smile that showcased deep dimples, dark, curly hair that he wore cropped short into a fade cut, and a rock-hard body that women craved. Destiny exhaled when Eric released her from the hug and said, "Thanks, Eric. You look great yourself." Eric only nodded and rubbed Destiny's back.

As usual, Destiny's family had a huge celebration for the 4th of July, but this year, it was special. Althea, Queen, and Maggie prepared the meats for the grill: chicken, a small pig that would be put into the pit and smoked, and smoked turkey legs. There were also potato salad, baked beans, coleslaw, corn on the cob, green beans, fried fish, fruit salad, cake, beer for the adults, and sodas and iced tea for the children. The day was filled with fun; the Blues were blaring on the jukebox; and the kids were playing Frisbee, hopscotch, and horseshoes. The adults were engaged in games of dominoes and chess on one side of the yard, and a few guys were playing spades and bid whist on the other side. Destiny was sitting at the table playing a game of checkers with her Uncle Jesse.

Uncle Jesse asked Destiny, "Baby girl, are you home to stay or just visiting?"

Destiny looked at Uncle Jesse, smiled, and said, "I am here for a month to visit Mama and enjoy the family."

Uncle Jesse looked across the yard to the card table where Eric sat playing spades and said, "Destiny, you left some unfinished business back here. That truly requires your attention before you leave!"

Destiny followed Uncle Jesse's eyes to Eric and said, "Eric and I are friends and have been for many years. I see no reason to change that now. Our friendship will go the distance."

Uncle Jesse patted Destiny's hand and said, "Baby girl, be careful. Make sure that you both are on the same page."

Destiny rose from the game, kissed Uncle Jesse on the cheek, and said, "I love you, Uncle Jesse. Thanks for the advice."

Destiny was not going to admit to her Uncle Jesse that each time she was near Eric, her stomach felt as if butterflies were dancing inside it. Her heartbeat would race just a little faster, and she enjoyed having him around. Destiny thought, *Oh my goodness, when did I start seeing Eric as more than my friend? Truth be told, the guy looks amazing! I have to get control of myself. Eric is my best friend, nothing more!*

Eric looked up from the card game and saw Destiny walking in their direction. Eric stood from the table and walked to meet Destiny with a huge smile on his face.

Eric asked, "Destiny, would you like something to drink? I was going to get a soda."

Destiny replied, "Sure, I will walk with you to get an iced tea."

Eric could not keep his eyes off Destiny. Destiny wore a pair of denim overall shorts, with a red tank top under them, minimal makeup, and gold tiny hoop earrings. A pair of red wedge sandals adorned her feet.

Eric was close enough to Destiny to inhale the fragrance that she wore, and he inquired, "What are you wearing?"

Destiny gave Eric a confused look and said, "What?"

Eric said, "The scent that you are wearing smells nice. What is it called?"

Destiny looked at Eric and said, "White Diamonds."

Eric nodded, and he and Destiny walked to the cooler and retrieved their individual drinks. Eric and Destiny were walking back in the direction of the domino table when he caught her hand, turned her to face him, and said, "Destiny, when you get some time, I would like to speak with you about an important matter." Destiny nodded and walked away to finish her game of checkers with Uncle Jesse.

Later that evening, after Destiny and her entire family and friends had enjoyed their 4th of July festivities and everyone was enjoying the soft music playing on the jukebox, Eric asked Destiny, "Will you please walk with me?" Destiny nodded yes. Eric grabbed Destiny's hand, and they began their slow walk to the area located at the back of the property, where a small brook tinkled water and the cicadas chirped.

Eric said, "Destiny, I brought you here because there is something that I would like to share with you. I realized it has been over a year since we have seen each other, but I have a confession to make. The reason I moved away to Dallas was twofold. The first reason was to attend the university as we discussed, but the main reason was I found myself starting to feel differently about you."

Destiny was glad it was dark, and Eric could not see her face because her cheeks were very flushed. Destiny said in a calm voice, "Eric, I am not sure I understand what you meant by the second reason you left. Please explain in detail."

Eric let out a sigh and began by saying, "Destiny, I had developed feelings for you over the years that were greater than friendship, and I wasn't sure how to deal with those feelings. Furthermore, I wasn't sure if you felt the same way about me as I did you. Destiny, I had fallen in love with you!"

Destiny sat there and pondered what Eric had just told her. Finally, Destiny turned to Eric and stated, "Eric, why did you leave instead of telling me the truth a year ago? Eric, had I known how you felt about me then, I would not have left and joined the military. Eric, I have a confession to make as well. My feelings were starting to grow for you. I got nervous and left. I didn't want to jeopardize our friendship."

Eric asked, "Destiny, is there any possibility that we may see each other while you are here? I am willing to give this relationship a try. Are you?"

Destiny said, "Eric, let's take things one day at a time and see where we go from there."

That was not the answer Eric wanted to hear, but he knew that was the best answer that Destiny would give for the time being. Destiny and Eric walked back to the gathering and helped the smaller children shoot their fireworks. Destiny bid Eric good night and went in the house to help Althea put away the food.

That night after everyone had long gone to sleep, Destiny lay on her bed thinking about the conversation she had earlier with Eric. Destiny thought, *Would it be selfish of me to explore my feelings for Eric when I am only going to be here for one month? What happens if the relationship actually works? Would Eric be willing to give up his career to follow me? God knows I am not willing to give up a career that I have just begun and move to Texas.* On the other side of town, Eric was also tossing and turning, wondering if he had made the right choice by telling Destiny how he felt. *Hell, what if she doesn't feel the same way I feel? What if she isn't willing to give us a chance? Would she give up the military for me?*

The next day dawned sunny and hot. Destiny awoke to the smells of bacon, eggs, sausage, pancakes, potatoes, grits, and biscuits with gravy. Destiny threw back the covers, got out of bed, made her bed, took a shower, and dressed in a pair of tattered jeans, a canary-yellow sleeveless shirt, and yellow sneakers. Destiny made her way to the kitchen and snatched a piece of bacon from the plate.

Destiny gave her mom a hug and a light peck on the cheek, saying, "Good morning, Mama."

Althea smiled and replied, "Good morning, baby girl. How did you sleep last night?"

Destiny smiled and said, "I slept well, Mama."

Althea told Destiny, "Wash your hands and set the table. I am sure your brother and cousins will be down soon."

Destiny did as she was told. As soon as the table was set, the entire kitchen filled with laughter and love. Jerry, Destiny's brother, came in, with her cousins Thomas, Levi, Joshua, and Jimmy. They all heaped food on their plates and ate like they were starved to death. Althea looked at the boys and said, "I am always happy for you all to visit. At least someone enjoys my cooking."

After breakfast, Destiny helped Althea clean the kitchen.

Althea noticed that Destiny had been very quiet at breakfast, so she inquired, "Destiny, is everything alright?"

Destiny looked at Althea with unshed tears in her eyes and said, "Mama, for the first time in my life, I don't know what to do!"

Althea looked at Destiny and said, "Destiny, you know you can talk to me about anything. What is going on that has you so confused?"

Destiny said, "Mama, I left home over a year ago, because I had to find myself and I also had to figure out how I felt about Eric. I thought that by my leaving, not being in a close proximity to him would help me clear my head. I have to admit that worked until I came home and saw him."

Althea took Destiny's hand and said, "Destiny, I was wondering how long it would take you two to figure out what was going on. Honey, we all saw the signs, and we were hopeful that the two of you would stop fighting the love that was blossoming between you. Love is one of the strongest emotions that anyone can experience. Love is patient and understanding; love provides hope, and it is caring; love is kind, and it will be your protector; love is meant to be shared. Destiny, the heart knows the direction that it wants to travel. Trust your heart and allow it to guide you in the right direction. Give Eric and love a chance."

Destiny dried her eyes and said, "Mama, thank you."

Althea watched her youngest walk from the kitchen with a heavy heart, because she was afraid to let go and let love have an opportunity to flourish.

Later that evening, while Destiny was sitting in her room listening to music, her phone rang; and it was Eric.

Destiny said, "Hello, Eric, how are you?"

Eric asked, "Destiny, are you busy right now? How would you like to go to the movies with me?"

Destiny replied, "Sure, Eric, I would like that very much. What time shall I expect you?"

Eric said, "Eight thirty, since the movie starts at nine."

Eric arrived at the Drakes' home promptly at eight thirty that evening and rang the doorbell.

Destiny opened the door, preparing to leave, but Eric asked Destiny, "Is it okay for me to say hello to Ms. Althea before we leave?"

Destiny smiled and said, "Mama would like that very much, Eric."

Eric spoke to Althea and gave her a hug, and he and Destiny left for the movies.

Eric and Destiny arrived at the theater at eight forty-seven. The two movies that Destiny and Eric were trying to decide between were *The Karate Kid II* and *Psycho III*, and Destiny chose *The Karate Kid II*. They got a tub of popcorn and two medium cokes and entered theater 5 for the showing of the movie. Eric held Destiny's hand through the entire movie, and as they were leaving the theater, he put his arm around Destiny while they walked to the car.

Eric asked Destiny, "Would you like to grab a bite to eat before we go home?"

Destiny said, "No, I am fine, Eric. Thanks for asking."

Eric drove Destiny home, got out, opened Destiny's door, helped her out of the vehicle, and walked her to the door. Once Destiny got to the door, she turned to Eric to say good night; and Eric pulled Destiny into his arms and kissed her long, hard, and passionately before he said good night. Eric then stepped from the porch, got in his car, waited for Destiny to secure the door, and drove home.

Destiny went straight to her room, since it was past midnight and her mother was fast asleep. Once in her room, Destiny brushed her teeth and prepared for bed.

Destiny was tired, but sleep would not come, for she was caught in the throes of the kiss she had shared with Eric. Destiny thought, *Oh my goodness, why did I wait so long to kiss Eric? If I had known it would have been that great to kiss him, I would have taken the liberty to kiss him earlier.* She drifted off to sleep with thoughts of Eric and "that kiss" on her mind.

Across town, Eric was having difficulty going to sleep as well. He lay on the bed thinking about how great Destiny felt in his arms and how good it felt to finally kiss her. Eric had to admit the kiss he shared with Destiny earlier tonight was far greater than how he had imagined it would be. Eric decided, *I have only one month to make Destiny love me, and I am going to give 100 percent to making my dream a reality!* Eric fell asleep thinking of Destiny and how much he loved her.

Finally, the weekend had arrived. Destiny spent Saturday with Althea. Destiny and Althea went shopping at the mall, in search of a nice dress for Destiny to wear to church on Sunday. After spending three hours walking through store after store, Destiny walked into *Dillard's* and found the perfect dress. The sheath dress was peach in color, had a pleated fitted bodice, was mid-length (just above the knee), and had a pearl and lace décolletage. Destiny had fallen in love and was determined that she would have that particular dress. There was only one dress left, and it was in Destiny's size, a size 10. Destiny purchased the dress along with a pair of sandals and a purse that would accessorize the dress. Destiny was not quite finished with her shopping spree just yet. She and Althea walked to *Macy's*, and Destiny saw the perfect dress for Althea. The dress was teal in color, silk in fabric, and pleated with wrap style. Destiny knew Althea would be a "dream" in that dress. Destiny found Althea's size and asked, "Mama, would you please try this dress on?" Althea was hesitant to do so, due to the price of the dress; but Destiny coaxed her to the dressing room, with the dress in hand. Althea was so excited about the feel of the fabric, as well as the way the dress was made. Althea tried the dress on and was surprised at the way it accentuated her figure. The dress was "perfect" in every way. Destiny purchased the teal dress, matching jewelry, shoes, and a handbag for Althea. Althea began to protest by saying, "Destiny, that is too much money to spend for one dress!" Destiny smiled, hugged Althea, and handed the saleslady her bank card for the purchases. Destiny and Althea left the mall and went home.

Destiny and Althea arrived home at five thirty that evening to find Eric sitting talking to Jerry and Uncle Jesse. When Destiny and Althea stepped out of the car with the packages, Eric left the porch to assist them with the bags. Eric took the bags from Destiny's hands and carried them all inside for her, stopping to kiss Althea on the cheek. Althea went inside, changed into her purple and green house dress, and began preparations for tonight's supper and Sunday's dinner.

Althea prepared supper, which consisted of hamburgers with pickles, lettuce, onions, tomatoes, and cheese. There were also hotdogs with potato wedges, baked beans, and coleslaw. Eric stayed for dinner. Eric could not keep his eyes off Destiny as he sat across the table trying to enjoy the terrific meal Althea had prepared.

After dinner was over, Althea said, "Destiny, I need some flour to make the chicken and dumplings for dinner tomorrow. Could you and Eric go to the store for me?"

Destiny asked Eric, "Would you like to ride with me to the store?"

Eric said, "Sure, Destiny, I would love to."

And of course, Althea said, "Take your time, because the chicken and dumplings are the last dish I am preparing this evening." Eric understood the message. "You two get out of this house and enjoy your time together and bring back the flour when you come."

Eric smiled and nodded at Althea saying, "Yes, ma'am, Ms. Althea."

Eric and Destiny went to the local *Kroger* store and picked up ten pounds of bleached flour for Althea, and then Eric and Destiny left. Eric and Destiny drove to Cutter's Point, a beautiful spot that overlooked the city, and sat there watching the sunset and talked.

Eric finally asked, "Destiny, would you be willing to leave the military if our relationship became serious?"

Destiny gave the question serious consideration before answering and then said, "Eric, at this point in my career, I must say no. I enjoy the job that I do. Eric, I am fighting for a cause that is greater than either of us. I am fighting for justice and freedom. I'm fighting for our way of life!"

Eric was not at all happy with Destiny's response, so he started the car and drove them home.

Eric pulled the car into Destiny's driveway, turned to her, and said, "Destiny, I was hoping that you would understand that I am seriously in love with you and I am ready to be married."

Destiny looked at Eric and said, "Eric, I am flattered that you have shared your true feelings with me, but I also find it selfish of you to expect me to give up my career for a life with you. If the roles were reversed, would you be willing to give up your career to follow me?"

Eric gave the question careful thought, and then he mumbled, "No, I would not. Asking me to do this would be equivalent to asking me to become dependent upon you for survival financially, and that I will not do!"

Destiny sat there for a moment, and then she looked at Eric and replied, "Eric, you have made it clear how you feel. I think it is best for us to terminate this relationship and remain friends. Some things are not meant to be."

Destiny did not wait for Eric to answer. She opened the door, got out of the car, and walked into her home, never looking back.

Destiny spent the next two weeks of her vacation with her family, refusing to take Eric's calls, thus preventing him from visiting her. Althea noticed that Destiny was quiet and that Eric had not been around for a while.

Althea inquired, "Destiny, is everything okay with you and Eric?"

Destiny explained, "Mama, as much as I care about Eric, I now know we can only be friends. Eric expects me to give up my career in order to be with him, and that I will not do!"

Althea pulled Destiny into her arms and gave her a motherly hug stating, "Destiny, you are your father's daughter, no doubt. As stubborn as he ever was, bless his heart. Baby, I am proud of you and the woman whom you have become. I love you, Destiny."

Part 3

Finally, it was time for Destiny to return to Korea and her career. Destiny said a tearful goodbye to her mother at the airport and boarded the plane with the knowledge that all was well in her life and with her family. Sixteen hours later, Destiny arrived at her destination, eager to get back to work. Colonel Thornton had arranged for the duty driver to pick Destiny up at the airport. Destiny returned home to the barracks, unpacked her suitcase, showered, set her alarm, and went to sleep. Destiny's alarm went off and startled her; but she crawled out of bed, dressed for physical training, and greeted her day with a smile. She was excited to get back to a "normal" lifestyle.

After physical training, Sergeant First Class (SFC) Jessup, Destiny's platoon sergeant, informed her that her expertise would be required on a night maneuver that the entire platoon was going on that night.

Destiny asked, "SFC Jessup, have you spoken to Colonel Thornton about my participation in the maneuver tonight?"

SFC Jessup replied, "SPC Drake, please pack your gear and be ready to move out tonight at 2300 hours."

"SFC Jessup, may I remind you that I am the only person whom Colonel Thornton has to perform his communication and maintain the office. If I participate in this maneuver, then I will not be able to perform my duties in support of Colonel Thornton's office."

SFC Jessup said, "*Enough, SPC Drake! You will be there tonight,* and that is the end of this discussion!"

SPC Drake said, "Understood, SFC Jessup. I will see you at 2300 hours."

Destiny showered, dressed in uniform, and reported to the brigade for work.

Colonel Thornton asked Destiny, "SPC Drake, how was your leave? Did you enjoy the time with your family?"

Destiny smiled, remembering the great time with her family, especially her mother, and said, "Yes, sir, I did."

Colonel Thornton briefed Destiny on all that she had missed during the month that she was gone. He also informed her that SFC Jessup wanted her to maintain communications for his maneuver that was taking place that night at 2300. The plan was for Destiny to load the equipment with a communication security (COMSEC) key, set up the equipment, and ensure that it was functioning properly; and Destiny would return to her barracks so that she could be ready to perform her daily duties for Colonel Thornton the next day.

Destiny reported to the platoon office at 2230 hours, so that she could help SFC Jessup with the communications equipment. At 2300 hours, all the communications equipment was loaded on the vehicle, and Destiny secured the communication keys upon her person.

SPC Drake asked, "SFC Jessup, where am I riding?"

SFC Jessup informed SPC Drake, "You will be my driver, and your duty will be radio dispatch personnel. You will be required to be with me during the maneuver."

Destiny replied, "Yes, SFC Jessup."

SFC Jessup had a formation with the platoon at 2330, informing each person who was riding where, who was riding with whom, and what was expected of each person once they reached their destination. At 2345, the platoon departed to the designated point for their assigned mission.

The platoon arrived at their destination about seventy-five minutes later. The area that SFC Jessup had chosen was rich, moist farmland, which had been purchased by the military. The location was ideal for training because the troops would be able to train in the manner as they would if attacked by their enemy. The area was located about ten or so miles from the Korean Demilitarized Zone (a strip of land running across the Korean Peninsula).

Everyone took their individual position and was marching to their objective, with SFC Jessup leading the way and SPC Drake to his right. SFC Jessup took two thirty-inch steps. SPC Drake was in step with him, when all of a sudden, there was a slight "popping noise." SFC Jessup yelled to his platoon, "*Retreat. Take cover!*" Everyone with the exception of SFC Jessup and SPC Drake retreated, and there was a bright flash; and then a spray of liquid hit SFC Jessup and SPC Drake in the face, chest, back, and their entire upper extremities. SPC Drake radioed, "We are under attack and request backup immediately! I repeat. We are under attack, and I request backup immediately. Please respond!" SPC Drake felt a burning sensation on the lower part of her face (where her helmet did not shield from the spray), her chest, and her back. SFC Jessup grabbed SPC Drake, threw her body to the ground, and shielded her with his own body. That was the last thing that SPC Drake remembered. That fateful night changed her life forever.

SPC Drake awoke to find First Sergeant Christian and Colonel Thornton sitting in her room.

SPC Drake asked, "What are you all doing in my room?"

Colonel Thornton looked at SPC Drake with unshed tears in his eyes and said, "SPC Drake, you are in the hospital. You have been here for four days now, and we have been waiting for you to wake up!"

Destiny could feel bandages on her face, chest, and back. Each time the First Sergeant and Colonel looked at her, it was with pity and/or pain in their eyes. Destiny asked, "Where is SFC Jessup?"

First Sergeant informed her, "SFC Jessup had to fly back stateside to Walter Reed Hospital."

SPC Drake then asked, "What about the rest of my platoon?"

Colonel Thornton informed her, "SPC Drake, we lost fifteen members of your platoon, and the rest to include you and SFC Jessup are critically wounded."

SPC Drake began to pray and cry for the lost members of her platoon, and the salty tears burned her wounds. SPC Drake asked the nurse, "Would you please hand me a mirror so that I may see the extent of my wounds?" The nurse had just picked up the mirror and was preparing to hand it to SPC Drake when the chaplain walked into the room and said these words to Destiny, "Soldier, let us pray. There is no wound too deep for God to heal and no problem too hard for *him* to handle!" SPC Drake took the Chaplain's hand as he led them into prayer. He prayed for Destiny's wounds to heal, for peace, and for the souls of the fifteen soldiers who were lost that fateful night.

Three weeks later, SPC Drake's bandages were removed. SPC Drake was not prepared for what she witnessed. Destiny's face was a mass of blisters where beautiful skin once existed. There were blisters and craters where skin had melted from her face and stuck to the bandages. SPC Drake was not able to look at her own reflection. For eight weeks after the bandages were removed, Destiny went through procedure after procedure, skin grafting, and laser surgery to repair the damages that had been done that fateful night. Doctors were baffled by what they saw, for they could not imagine what could have caused this extensive damage. Finally, Colonel Thornton ordered that SPC Drake be flown to a specialty hospital that dealt in reconstructive surgery for extensive injuries. SPC Drake spent six additional weeks there, having procedures done that corrected her face, but still there would be scarring and damaged tissue. SPC Drake thanked God that she was alive, despite the damages that she had sustained.

Six months later, SPC Drake returned to duty, the scars were visible, but healing was taking place. Colonel Thornton was glad to see her, and he tried to shield SPC Drake from as much criticism as possible. SPC Drake performed her duties in a proficient and professional manner until it was time for her tour to end.

Everywhere that SPC Drake went, people would gawk at her as if she was some sort of a freak. One day, a young man saw SPC Drake walking on the street, and he said, "What the hell happened to her? She looks like some type of a freak from the circus!" SPC Drake squared her shoulders, held her head high, and continued to walk in the direction she was going, as if she had not heard his comment. At the same time, a little boy with an ice-cream cone had heard the man's comment. The little boy walked up to Destiny and said, "I do not think you are ugly. I like you just the way God made you!" The little boy gave Destiny a big hug and ran to catch up with his friends. At that moment, Destiny cried her first tear, not for what had happened to her nor the injuries that she was suffering from. The tear that she shed was a "tear of joy," because she was humbled to see that one person could show her so much love when yet another person showed so much malice and hate. Destiny realized that God had spared her life for a reason, and she was glad to be alive. The scars she carried were minimal in comparison to the lives lost, and for that she was thankful to be alive.

CHAPTER 3

Recovery

Destiny Drake had encountered some recent trials and tribulations in her life. She had had to overcome the death of her fellow soldiers, the pain of a life-altering event, and the despair of moving to a new duty station, within ten months. Destiny grew up in the church and had always been a praying woman. She knew that when life became tough and at the darkest point in her life, she had to remain prayerful, keep her faith, and depend on God. It was faith that had sustained her these past months, and it was God's grace that encouraged her to persevere.

Destiny had received PCS orders to Fort Gordon, Georgia, where she was relocated to the 15th Signal Brigade. Destiny was assigned to work in the communication center, processing classified messages and maintaining classified equipment. This job was one that Destiny was comfortable performing, and she was very proficient at her duties. SFC LeVoe was impressed with Destiny's work ethics and was considering sending SPC Drake to COMSEC class.

SPC Drake informed SFC LeVoe, "I have already attended the course and am presently certified to issue, reproduce, distribute, and load COMSEC material as required."

SFC LeVoe asked Destiny, "Are you familiar with all the processes required to reinitialize the COMSEC equipment?"

SPC Drake nodded the affirmative.

Four months after arriving to the 15th Signal Brigade, SPC Drake was promoted to the rank of sergeant. With Destiny's promotion, there were additional responsibilities that she was expected to perform.

SFC LeVoe informed Destiny, "You are second in command. When I am absent, you are expected to maintain the office as well as the soldiers."

Sergeant (SGT.) Drake stated, "I understand, SFC LeVoe, and which soldiers will I be required to counsel?"

SFC LeVoe explained, "You are responsible for counseling all four soldiers who work in this office, and I will counsel you."

Sergeant Drake noticed that everyone in the office was staring at her face; but only one person, Private (PV2) Jones, had the decency to ask, "Sergeant Drake, what happened to your face?"

Sergeant Drake stated, "I am only going to tell the story one time, so I suggest everyone listen. My platoon went on a night maneuver; we were attacked both chemically and physically. There were fatalities as well as casualties that night. We lost fifteen members from our platoon, and my platoon sergeant and I were critically injured."

PV2 Jones said, "I am so sorry that you were attacked, sergeant. You are a pretty woman."

Sergeant Drake smiled and said, "Thank you, PV2 Jones, for the compliment."

PFC Tyson asked, "May I touch your face, the scars I mean?"

Destiny said, "I would prefer that you don't touch my face. It is still tender and sensitive to the touch."

Destiny's promotion to a Noncommissioned Officer (NCO) required her to move to the NCO living quarters. Destiny moved into her new living quarters with the help of her supervisor, SFC LeVoe, and her new soldiers. Destiny worked to make the quarters her home by adding pictures of her and the family, removing the military furniture, and purchasing furniture of her own choosing. All in all, the place was quite cozy, a place that Destiny was proud of.

Destiny had two neighbors, both males, SSG Devon Peterson and SSG Charles Pierce; both were assigned to the Fifteenth Signal

Brigade but worked in different areas than Destiny worked. Devon always seemed to be in the kitchen at the same time that Destiny was preparing her meals. Destiny would prepare her meal and sit at the table in the dining area to enjoy it. Once she was finished with her meal, she would make sure to clean the dishes that she had utilized preparing her meal and sweep and mop the kitchen. She would even empty the trash if it was full when she finished cleaning the kitchen.

One Sunday afternoon, Destiny had a taste for pork chops, rice with mushroom gravy, corn on the cob, green beans, apple turnovers, salad, rolls, and iced tea. She spent the afternoon preparing this meal; and by the time she was finished, Devon, Charles, and three others from her floor were in the kitchen asking, "My goodness, what are you cooking that smells so heavenly? Is it possible that you have enough food to share?"

Destiny smiled and said, "Here's the deal. I will share the food only if you all wash the dishes, sweep and mop the kitchen floor, and empty the trash."

Devon and Charles agreed to perform the menial tasks in exchange for dinner with Destiny. They sat at the dining table and enjoyed the food while getting to know each other. From that point forward, Devon, Charles, and Troy would always offer to take Destiny to the store to shop for food, oftentimes contributing to the monies for groceries, in exchange for a decent meal.

Finally, the holidays were drawing near, and Destiny had decided to stay in Georgia for Thanksgiving, rather than go home. Destiny decided to cook dinner and invite her soldiers over to eat. She roasted a turkey, made stuffing from scratch, and had green beans, corn on the cob, mashed potatoes, chocolate cake, cranberry sauce, sweet potato pie, iced tea, and dinner rolls. PV2 Jones was the only soldier who wasn't going to dinner with her co-workers.

Destiny asked, "PV2 Jones, what are you doing for Thanksgiving? Has anyone invited you over for dinner?"

PV2 Jones said, "Sergeant, SFC LeVoe invited me over, but I declined, since everyone else from work was going there."

Destiny said, "I understand, but I can't have you sitting in your room alone on the holiday. I am cooking dinner for myself and three other NCOs. Please come have dinner with me. I would love to have you over."

PV2 Jones accepted Destiny's invitation and asked, "What would you like for me to bring, sergeant?"

Destiny said, "Just bring yourself and your appetite!"

They both laughed and went home.

Thanksgiving morning dawned bright and cold. Destiny was up before dawn so that she could prepare and season the turkey and put it in the oven to bake. She then began to cook the sweet potatoes so that she could make the sweet potato pies. After the pies were made and put into the second oven, Destiny began cutting the vegetables to make the stuffing. Destiny had made the stuffing and was getting ready to put it in the oven when Devon came sauntering in the kitchen. He asked, "What is it that I can do to help with dinner?" Destiny informed him that the pies were ready to come out of the oven. Devon took the pies from the oven and sat them on the counter to cool. He then checked the turkey to make sure it was okay. Destiny and Devon worked in harmony to complete the Thanksgiving dinner, and they were proud of their accomplishments.

Destiny said, "Thanks, Devon, for all your help in preparing this meal."

Devon smiled and said, "It was my pleasure, Destiny. You did the most of the work."

By two o'clock, the dinner was cooked, everyone had changed into their holiday attire, and the table was set with beautiful dishes that Destiny had found in the cabinets.

PV2 Jones offered to say grace, "Dear Lord, thank you for this magnificent meal. Thank you for Sergeant Drake and keep each and every one safe this day!"

Destiny said, "Amen."

Destiny, PV2 Jones, Devon, Troy, and Tristan ate their dinner. Destiny served the potato pie after everyone had eaten their fill of the turkey and fixings. Destiny provided take-home plates for PV2 Jones and stored the remainder of the food in the refrigerator for the next day.

At about five o'clock that evening, Destiny called home.

Destiny told Althea, "Mama, I cooked dinner today for people in my barracks and one of my soldiers. I cooked your sweet potato pie the way you had showed me to make it, and everyone loved it. Mama, I miss you so much! Give my love to everyone, and I hope to see you on Christmas."

Althea asked, "Destiny, is everything okay? Baby, I know about the incident. Colonel Thornton called and told me what happened. I want you to know that I will always love you no matter what. I love you, baby, and I hope to see you soon."

Destiny cried after hanging up from talking to Althea, because she realized it was so silly of her to not go home, all because she was worried about her family seeing her with all the scars.

The day after Thanksgiving, Destiny decided it was time for a new wardrobe. She got dressed and went to the mall. She found several beautiful pieces that she liked, but she also used the time to complete her Christmas shopping as well. She bought a beautiful red dress with long sleeves, a slit in the back, silky fabric, fitted waist, and cowl neckline. Destiny bought the dress with the thought of wearing it for the holidays when she went home. She also bought a cute sweater dress, mahogany colored, knee length, and fitted. The dress had beautiful brass buttons that started at the neckline and ended at the waist. Destiny purchased a pair of black boot-type shoes to go with that dress. Destiny made a few more purchases, and then she went home.

Destiny returned to her living quarters, stored her packages, and was just sitting down to watch television when there was a knock on her door. Destiny opened the door, expecting to see one of her neighbors standing there; but she was truly surprised to see SFC Jessup standing at her door.

Destiny screamed and said, "SFC Jessup, it is so great to see you. For a minute, I thought my eyes were playing tricks on me. Please come in. Oh my goodness, how have you been?"

SFC Jessup said, "I have been well. After getting out of the hospital, I was reassigned to Fort Gordon. I had heard that you were here, but I wasn't sure if you were ready to relive that 'fateful night' yet. How have you been, Sergeant Drake? You look wonderful."

Destiny said, "Thank you, SFC Jessup, not just for the compliment, but for saving my life that night. I know had it not been for you, I might not have been here today!"

SFC Jessup replied, "It was the least that I could do. It was my fault that you were on that mission; I had to ensure that I had the best operator for my communications if anything went wrong."

Destiny and SFC Jessup sat in silence for a moment, both remembering the ordeal that they had experienced.

Finally, SFC Jessup spoke, "I heard from Colonel Thornton a couple of days ago. Sergeant Drake, he told me you were here and asked me to check on you. I have something for you." SFC Jessup handed Destiny a slip of paper. That paper contained the name and number of Colonel Thornton, and to Destiny's surprise, it was a local number.

Destiny immediately called the number, and she heard a familiar voice say, "Hello, Sergeant Drake, I see that you got your surprise!"

Destiny began to shed tears of joy and said, "Thank you, Colonel Thornton, for the wonderful surprise. I am so happy to see SFC Jessup and to know that I have someone here whom I consider family, you and SFC Jessup!"

Destiny could hear the happiness in his voice. Colonel Thornton invited Destiny to have coffee. He wanted to see how his soldier was doing, as well as find out how she was settling in at her new duty station.

Sunday morning arrived, and Destiny awoke feeling blessed. She prepared toast and tea for breakfast and then dressed for church. Destiny chose a midnight-blue pinstripe skirt suit, with a sky-blue blouse to wear with it. She wore silver earrings, a silver bangle bracelet that her mother had given her for her twenty-second birthday, a silver watch, and blue pumps. Destiny removed the pins from her hair and fluffed her curls until they hung to her shoulders, bouncy, shiny, and free. Destiny took one last glance in the mirror, grabbed her purse, and left her quarters.

Destiny arrived at church in record time and went inside and found a seat. Destiny was just preparing to be seated after the morning hymn when a well-dressed gentleman walked to her seat and asked, "May I sit here?" Destiny turned to see Colonel Thornton standing there. She turned and hugged him, moving down to make room for him on the pew. Destiny knew at that moment God had truly sent her a blessing.

During the church services, the pastor asked, "Is there any person here who can testify about God's goodness, grace, and mercy? If so, please come forward!" Destiny could feel the spirit moving within her body: She began to get this warm sensation spread throughout her body, her feet began to get light, and before she knew it, she had stood up and was walking to the front of the church. Destiny said, "I thank God for *his* love, *his* mercy, and *his* grace. I am a soldier; and ten months ago, while on a mission, my platoon and I came under attack. We were attacked both physically and chemically. We lost fifteen members of our team that night, and I was critically injured, sustaining major damage to my face and body. But God intervened and made it possible for people to care enough about me to ensure that I received the best care possible. I thank *him* first for sparing my life, I thank *him* for placing caring people in my life, and I thank *him* for the surgeons who made it possible for my face to heal as well as it has, scars and all." There was not a dry eye in the church when Destiny finished testifying that morning, to include Colonel Thornton. The pastor hugged Destiny and said a prayer, ending church services.

Colonel Thornton hugged Destiny and invited her to lunch. They went to lunch at the country club.

Colonel Thornton asked Destiny, "How have you been?"

Destiny replied, "I have been well, keeping busy with work and adjusting to my new position." Destiny looked at Colonel Thornton and said, "Colonel Thornton, I want to thank you for all that you did for me when I was hurt. I know that you made sure that I had the best medical care that was possible. I now know that you sent me to some of the best medical facilities known for the injuries I sustained. I thank you.

Colonel Thornton said, "Sergeant Drake, you are most welcome. If I had a daughter, I would want her to be like you."

Destiny said, "Thank you, sir. How long have you been here?"

Colonel Thornton then explained to Destiny, "I knew that I was coming here shortly before your incident. So after you and SFC Jessup were injured, I made a few phone calls to ensure that we all could be stationed together here at Fort Gordon."

Destiny said, "I see. Thank you."

They finished their lunch, Destiny hugged Colonel Thornton and thanked him for lunch, and each went their separate ways.

It was mid-December, and Destiny was taking leave to go home. She shipped all her presents in advance to ensure that they would arrive ahead of her. She also called ahead warning, "No one is to open his or her present until Christmas morning."

Three days before Christmas, Destiny arrived at the airport in Little Rock. Her family was waiting to greet her, once again. When Destiny saw Althea, she ran to her and hugged her tight, saying, "Mama, I missed you so much!" Althea hugged her daughter with tears in her eyes, for she was happy to see Destiny after all that she had been through. Althea needed the hug just as much as Destiny did, because it was assurance that her baby was alive and well!

The Drakes arrived home, Destiny unpacked, and Althea began her preparations for the evening meal. This time, Destiny helped Althea prepare dinner, both women working in harmony and creating a tasty meal. They prepared barbecued ribs, potato salad, baked beans, corn, and salad greens with cucumbers and tomatoes. They served iced tea and cola. Destiny had forgotten how good it felt to be home, enjoying time with the family.

At four o'clock on Christmas morning, the Drake family was up opening gifts and enjoying each other's company. After opening gifts, Althea prepared breakfast for her family; they ate breakfast and prepared for Sunrise Church services. As they were dressed for church services, Althea told Destiny, "I have a surprise for you, but you have to wait until we get to church, because your surprise is waiting for us at church. Let's go, baby." Destiny was curious and could hardly wait to get to church. She wondered, *How can I have a surprise at church? Did Mama invite someone here for the holidays and fail to inform me of having done so?*

Destiny and Althea arrived at church, they were greeted by everyone they knew, and they finally made their way to their family pew. And to Destiny's surprise, Colonel Thornton and SFC Jessup were already seated on the pew. Althea said, "Merry Christmas, baby." Destiny was so happy she couldn't contain herself; she gave a high-pitched scream, causing everyone to turn and stare at them. To Colonel Thornton and SFC Jessup, Althea said, "Good morning. Thanks for coming to spend the holidays with my family." Althea had called them as soon as she knew Destiny was coming home and invited both men to spend the holidays with her family, since neither of them had any family of their own. Althea was sure having Colonel Thornton and SFC Jessup would make Destiny feel better, since they were close friends of hers.

The holidays were filled with fun, festivities, and laughter. Destiny showed Michael Thornton and Terence Jessup around her quaint city, showing them the historical sites as well as the fun sights. Destiny was excited to have her two best friends home with her for the holidays. Althea would cook delightful meals ensuring that everyone had plenty of food to eat. They would all sit around the fireplace after supper, listening to Michael and Terence spinning tales of their adventures in the military. It was the best Christmas that Destiny had in quite some time. But it was time for Michael, Terence, and Destiny to bid the family goodbye and return to their duties, to protect the country and their freedom.

Destiny returned to work after the New Year and was informed that SFC LeVoe had an emergency and she was presently on emergency leave. Command Sergeant Major (CSM) Stevens requested an appointment with Destiny. Destiny was called into CSM Stevens's office at six thirty in the morning.

The conversation went something like this, "Sergeant Drake, I was informed by SFC LeVoe that you were highly trained and skilled in running the communication center. I expect you to be proficient at your job, ensuring my soldiers are taken care of; and if you have a problem, I expect you to come to me directly."

Destiny said, "CSM, I have everything under control. I am aware of the day-to-day operations. I am adept at issuing COMSEC, rekeying all classified equipment, initializing the system, performing over-the-air rekeying (OTAR) processes, as well as maintaining our customers' messages and internet traffic."

After Destiny had explained her qualifications, CSM Stevens only nodded, dismissing Destiny to the communication center to prepare for the daily operations.

Sergeant Drake spent eight weeks maintaining the communication center and the soldiers. Sergeant Drake performed the end-of-month destruction of COMSEC as required; she reissued COMSEC and reloaded all classified equipment within the brigade, to include performing four OTARs. Sergeant Drake was required to submit the monthly COMSEC report to the proper authorities and then report to CSM Stevens. Sergeant Drake performed all the duties that SFC LeVoe had performed, yet she was able to send two soldiers to the motor pool on Mondays for motor maintenance of her section's vehicle.

Two weeks later, CSM Stevens called the communication center and said, "Sergeant Drake, I need to see you in my office!"

Sergeant Drake politely informed CSM Stevens, "CSM Stevens, I apologize, but presently I am not able to come to your office. I have to be here at the office and issue keys to other personnel within the brigade." Destiny asked, "CSM Stevens, is it possible for you to come to the communication center and we discuss everything here?"

CSM wasn't happy with the information Sergeant Drake had just provided to him, so he informed Sergeant Drake, "I will be there in fifteen minutes, and I expect you to be out front waiting to escort me back to your facility."

Destiny replied, "Yes, CSM, I will await your arrival." Destiny then called Mr. Watson, the security personnel, and said, "Mr. Watson, could you please call me when CSM Stevens's vehicle arrives in the parking lot?"

Mr. Watson said, "Sergeant Drake, I will call you as soon as his driver pulls into the lot."

Sergeant Drake was waiting at the front desk, thanks to Mr. Watson, and she escorted CSM Stevens back. Sergeant Drake called into the communication center and informed PV2 Jones, "PV2

Jones, *sanitize!*" This was Sergeant Drake's way of informing PV2 Jones to cover all classified matter that was beyond CSM Stevens's security clearance level. PV2 Jones rang the phone outside the door and informed Sergeant Drake, "*All clear!*" This was an indication that all materials were secured and that Sergeant Drake could now bring CSM Stevens into the facility.

Sergeant Drake and CSM Stevens entered the facility. PV2 Jones and PFC Tyson left the facility, providing Destiny and CSM some privacy to talk. Destiny offered CSM Stevens her seat, and she stood at parade rest and listened to what CSM had to say. CSM said, "Sergeant Drake, I came here to inform you that SFC LeVoe is being reassigned to a duty station closer to her home, due to her emergency. She will be returning long enough to sign this facility and everything in it over to you. You will be responsible for maintaining 450 thousand dollars' worth of equipment and four soldiers, and you are now in charge of this facility as of today. We will inventory everything according to the hand receipts SFC LeVoe signed, and you will then sign for everything. By the way, you are getting promoted to the rank of Staff Sergeant next week. And at such time, you will take over everything!"

Sergeant Drake had five days to process everything, inventory all equipment, and maintain the communication center and her soldiers while inheriting SFC LeVoe's platoon as well. Destiny knew she had her work cut out for her.

Destiny asked CSM Stevens, "CSM Stevens, is it possible for me to make a request?" CSM Stevens nodded the affirmative. Destiny said, "CSM Stevens, I know a Sergeant First Class who would be willing to take SFC LeVoe's place. If you were willing to bring this individual on board as the platoon sergeant, I could maintain everything else."

CSM asked, "Who is this soldier whom you are talking about?"

Destiny replied, "SFC Terence Jessup, CSM."

CSM smiled, because he knew SFC Jessup and, for some reason, he never considered him for the position. CSM said, "Sergeant Drake, this is my recommendation. You are signing for everything, and SFC Jessup will be brought over as the platoon sergeant. Your responsibilities will remain the same, with the exception of the platoon."

Destiny was happy with CSM Stevens's decision, because she knew her duties and could perform them all. Destiny was not ready to become a platoon sergeant. She needed more guidance and mentoring. This she knew.

CSM Stevens was true to his word. Two days later SFC Jessup was assigned to the brigade as the new platoon sergeant for the first platoon. Sergeant Drake was responsible for ensuring that SFC Jessup had all the vital information concerning the facility in order to be productive as well as proficient. SFC Jessup shared the same Military Occupational Specialty as Destiny, so he understood everything that Destiny did in the communication center.

SFC Jessup was present for Destiny's promotion, but it was Colonel Thornton who pinned her new SSG stripes on her uniform. It was official; Destiny had earned yet another promotion, cementing her career.

Destiny was amazed at how her military career was progressing; but her only regret was that her father was not there to witness her success. She wished things would have been different all those years ago and her father could have survived the accident. But that was not the case. She had to accept that everything happened for a reason, even though she might not be aware of that reason; maybe it was part of God's overall plan for her. She finally realized there was no need to think about the "what ifs." She had to remain focused on the here and now. Destiny knew she was fortunate to have a loving mother who doted on her and was always proud of her accomplishments.

Destiny knew with this new promotion, there would be an added responsibility for her to manage. So far, she was feeling good at her job, the people she worked with, her soldiers, as well as the expectations that CSM Stevens had of her. To be honest, she had accomplished far more that she thought was possible in her short time in the military. Life had not always been easy, but had it been easy, she was sure she would not have been happy with her life.

SFC Jessup was in awe of Destiny and the intensity she brought to any assigned project. He was certain she had a bright future in the communication field, or any field for that matter.

SFC Jessup said, "SSG Drake, I am so proud of you and all that you have accomplished in such a short time."

Destiny said, "Thank you, SFC Jessup. I must admit I had a great teacher. Had you not pushed me to be the best that you knew I could be, none of this would have been possible."

SFC Jessup said, "SSG Drake, give yourself some of the credit. It was your determination, dedication to detail, and desire to succeed that has gotten you to this point. Don't ever sell yourself short, SSG Drake."

Destiny smiled and told SFC Jessup, "Now that we have everything in order, let's get out of here and go get us a bite to eat. It is my treat since I just got promoted."

SFC Jessup said, "You got it. Let's go!"

CHAPTER 4

Enchantment

The last year had been tumultuous for Destiny. Destiny had had to make several adaptations in her life. She had to adjust mentally, physically, and psychologically to the various obstacles that she had triumphed in the past year. Destiny understood the concept of "total person transformation." The past year hadn't been easy for Destiny, but it had been essential to her being able to accept herself, despite the perceptions that others might have concerning her.

Destiny had carved a niche for herself at the Fifteenth Signal Brigade and had proven to be a valuable member of the team. Destiny had improved communication processes by 60 percent within the brigade, and everyone was happy with the services that the communication center provided. SFC Jessup recommended Destiny for a commendation medal, and CSM Stevens ensured that the medal was awarded to her for the outstanding communication processes that she had made possible throughout the brigade. Destiny was modest about having been honored by the award; her opinion was she was performing her job to the utmost of her ability.

The weekend had finally arrived, and Destiny and her friend Tiffany (SSG Buckley) had plans to go dancing. After work, the two went to the mall to find an outfit to wear out to the club that night. Destiny chose a pair of black leggings, a red and black sheer tunic with slits on the sides, a red tank top, black boots, and gold earrings to accent the outfit. Tiffany chose midnight-blue straight leg pants, a blue and silver top that had a sheer panel down the back, and silver shoes. The two ladies paid for their purchases and returned to their quarters to ready themselves for their evening out. Once Tiffany was ready, she picked up Destiny, and they decided where they were going.

Tiffany and Destiny went to the Noncommissioned Officers' Club on post. The deejay was spinning the records, and everyone was on the floor dancing and having a good time. Tiffany was on the dance floor with a guy she knew, and they were grooving to the music. Destiny was sitting at the table sipping her drink when the deejay put on a slow song by the O'Jays, "Forever Mine," which was one of Destiny's all-time favorite songs. Destiny was listening to the first bars of the song when a tall, semi-dark, well-dressed gentleman came over to the table and said, "Would you like to dance?" Destiny answered "Yes," and she stood, and he escorted her to the dance floor. The gentleman was six feet and three inches tall, his skin was the color of toasted caramel, he had wavy black hair, and he smelled so good. The deejay didn't stop the "slow train" that he began. He continued with Shirley Murdock's "As We Lay." Destiny was prepared to walk back to her table when the gentleman, Vance Harmon, pulled Destiny close for another dance. Vance and Destiny danced the remainder of the night away, enjoying the slow songs that the deejay kept spinning one right after the other.

Vance was enjoying the time with Destiny, and most thought he was infatuated with her. After the bartender made the *last call for alcohol*, Vance asked Destiny, "May I have your phone number, so that I may call you?" Destiny gave Vance her phone number, but she was sure he would not call her. After all, who would seriously be interested in a woman with facial scars? Destiny was surprised he asked her to dance.

Destiny spent Saturday cleaning her quarters and doing laundry. After her chores were finished, she decided to get dressed and go to the Postal Exchange (PX) to look for her mother a birthday gift. Destiny first looked to see if the PX had any new arrivals in the clothes section; then she perused the store looking at various pieces of jewelry. She finally chose a diamond cross pendant, with a tiny, thin, gold chain to suspend it from, and also a pair of diamond stud earrings. Destiny paid for her purchases, left the store, and went home.

Just as Destiny was walking in her quarters, her phone rang, and she answered "Hello." Destiny heard Vance's deep voice resonate through the phone as he said, "Hello, may I speak to Destiny please?"

Destiny replied, "This is she; may I ask who is calling?"

Vance said, "This is Vance Harmon. We met at the NCO club last night."

Destiny smiled and said, "Hello, Vance, I do remember our meeting and dancing most of the night."

Vance and Destiny made small talk for a few minutes, and then Vance said, "Destiny, I called to see if you would be interested in having dinner with me tonight."

Destiny said, "Yes, I would like that very much."

Vance told her, "Our reservations are for eight o'clock. I will see you at ten past seven tonight."

Destiny asked, "How did you know I would say yes?"

Vance said, "I didn't, but I was hoping you would."

Vance had made reservations at *Cadwallader's*. Destiny was dressed for any occasion, especially for dinner at this elegant establishment. Destiny was wearing a fitted black dress with a slit in the back, gold and black strappy sandals, gold bangle bracelets, a gold necklace, and gold hoop earrings. She wore her hair in a beautiful updo style, and her makeup was flawless. She was a sight to behold, and Vance smiled, giving her an approving look.

Then he told her, "Destiny, you look beautiful tonight."

Destiny smiled and said, "Thank you."

Vance was dressed in a black suit, white shirt and black tie with tiny white dots, and black dress shoes. His only jewelry was a gold watch. His hair was still damp from his shower, and his hair was very wavy. Destiny and Vance ordered their drinks and made use of the time to get to know each other while waiting for their drinks to arrive. They continued their conversation over appetizers and then ordered their main course. Everything was flavorful and delicious.

Vance was a Sergeant First Class, working as a military police there on Fort Gordon. He had three brothers and one sister. His father was from Spain, and his mother was African-American. His parents had met when his father was in the military, and they married after having dated for one year. Vance was the eldest child, and he was twenty-eight years old.

After dinner, Vance and Destiny drove back to the *James Brown Arena* to watch a live play that Vance had gotten tickets for.

After the play was over and they were driving back to post, Destiny said, "Vance, thank you for a lovely evening. I truly enjoyed it."

Vance smiled and said, "You are welcome, and I too enjoyed this evening."

Destiny and Vance were enjoying each other's company after their first date.

They would spend their weekend's horseback riding, attending sports events, and cooking. They even spent one Saturday in Savannah, Georgia, visiting the *Skidaway Island State Park, Grayson Stadium,* and other historic sites in the old city. They enjoyed delectable treats and had a hearty dinner consisting of rich, flavorful food.

Destiny and Vance were enjoying the time they spent together. Their time was magical, and both Vance and Destiny hoped their time together would never end. That was not to be the case. Destiny's tour of duty in Fort Gordon was coming to a close.

Six months after having met Vance, Destiny received PCS orders to Heidelberg, Germany. Destiny finally gained the courage to tell Vance about her PCS orders, and he was heartbroken. Vance was not ready for Destiny to leave. Vance could not imagine the next year at Fort Gordon without her being there as well.

Destiny was not happy with the dilemma she found herself in, so she explained her predicament to Colonel Thornton, and he listened intently. It pained Colonel Thornton deeply to see the pain in Destiny's eyes at the thought of leaving the one she loved. Destiny was not ready to leave Fort Gordon now that she had met Vance. He knew that he had to do something to make this wrong right, so that Destiny could be happy again. Colonel Thornton missed seeing the gleam of happiness in Destiny's eyes, especially when she discussed having to leave Fort Gordon.

Finally Destiny had found someone whom she truly cared about. She had fallen in love with Vance Harmon. She was not quite sure when she relinquished ownership of her heart to Vance, but at some point, she allowed herself to fall deeply in love with this man; and she wasn't ready to give him up, not just yet!

Destiny knew that if her and Vance's relationship was destined to be, then this separation would only make their love grow stronger; but still she did not want to leave him. Each time she was near Vance, her heart sang to remain in his presence. Destiny knew that love was a powerful emotion and love could sustain the test of time. But she didn't want to test that theory if she didn't have to!

Destiny was a soldier, and she knew that wherever the Army needed her, that was where she would go. Destiny put her feelings aside and allowed the reality of the situation to prevail. She packed her belongings in preparation for her relocation to Heidelberg, Germany, preparing to leave her heart and Vance Harmon in Fort Gordon, Georgia. Once her quarters were cleared and her belongings shipped to Germany, Destiny took thirty days leave before going to Germany. Vance put in for leave as well, so that he could spend as much time with Destiny as possible before she left for Germany.

Vance had introduced Destiny to his family; and they all adored her, especially his younger sister, Stephanie. Vance's parents could see that their son was in love with Destiny, and it pained his mother to see her son unhappy. Vance's father spoke to him, explaining some of the options that were available. The best option would be to marry Destiny before she left, thus providing an alternative to the situation at hand. Armed with this information, Vance was ready to bring his plan to fruition.

Vance was ready to meet Destiny's family. Vance and Destiny flew to Arkansas so that he could meet Destiny's family. Destiny was nervous during the entire plane ride, for she wondered whether or not Althea would like Vance. Destiny was positive that once her mother saw how much she cared for Vance, everything would be fine.

As the plane was landing, Vance looked at Destiny and said, "Are you ready for this?"

Destiny smiled nervously and said, "Yes, I can't wait for you to meet my mother."

Vance had a hidden agenda that Destiny was not aware of. His reason for wanting to meet Destiny's family was simple; he had plans to ask Althea for permission to marry Destiny. He was positive that once Althea saw how much he loved her daughter, she would give them her blessing to wed. Furthermore, Vance was convinced that if he and Destiny were to marry, then they could be stationed together, which would be better than their being apart.

Destiny and Vance arrived in Little Rock, retrieved their luggage and rental car, and began their journey to Destiny's home. Destiny called Althea and said, "Mama, Vance and I just arrived in Little Rock. We rented a car, and we are driving down. We should be there soon. I love you." Althea was excited that Destiny had finally found someone who made her happy, and she couldn't wait to meet this young man.

Three hours later, Destiny and Vance arrived at the Drakes' home. Destiny introduced Vance to everyone, saving Althea for last to be introduced. Destiny was nervous about Althea's response, but when she introduced Althea to Vance, Althea hugged him and welcomed him to her home. Vance was so relieved that Althea was accepting of him, which would make things much easier when the time came.

As usual, Destiny brought her mother a gift. This time, she brought Althea a beautiful linen dress. The dress was burnt orange with pleats at the waist and a slight slit on the side, and the neckline was adorned with tiny seed pearls. Althea opened the wrapping that held the dress, folded it neatly, and laid it on the table. She carefully unfolded the dress and admired it for a moment. Then she hugged Destiny and said, "Thank you, baby. You always give me the most beautiful gifts. I love you so much!" Vance was humbled by the manner in which Althea received the gift that Destiny had brought. It was at that very moment that he realized Althea was truly a "woman of substance." He could see why Destiny was so loving and humble, yet she was a strong, beautiful woman. Destiny said, "Mama, would you please try the dress on so that I can see how it looks on you?" Althea was so excited about the dress and wanting to feel the fabric against her skin; Destiny didn't have to ask but once. Althea did as Destiny asked, and the dress fit her perfectly. The color of the dress accented Althea's skin color and picked up the gold flecks of her eyes. She was a beautiful sight to behold.

Althea changed back into her house dress and informed Destiny and Vance, "Dinner is almost ready." She also told Destiny, "Please show Vance to his room so that he can get ready for dinner." Destiny did as she was told. Destiny then went to her old room, showered, and changed for dinner. Vance wore jeans, a blue plaid button-down shirt, and some sneakers. Destiny wore jeans, a long-sleeved red tunic, and her reddish-brown boots. Althea had dinner on the table; she served roasted chicken, rice, broccoli, cream gravy, salad, carrots and sweet peas, dinner rolls, tea, and apple pie. Vance had a hearty appetite, and he sampled each dish on the table.

Vance said, "I see where Destiny gets her cooking skills. Everything is delicious."

Althea smiled and said, "Thank you, Vance."

After dinner, Destiny and Vance went for a walk. They walked down by the brook and watched the ducks swim on the water. It was a peaceful evening. They held hands and just enjoyed each other's company. Both understood the need to just "be"; no words were necessary.

As Althea was putting away the food and preparing to do dishes, the phone rang. Althea answered the phone.

Althea said, "Hello, Drake residence, Althea speaking. How may I help you?"

Colonel Thornton smiled as he heard Althea's voice and said, "Hello, Althea, this is Colonel Thornton. How are you doing?"

Althea smiled and said, "Colonel Thornton, it is good to hear your voice. I have been well. How have you been?"

Colonel Thornton and Althea exchanged pleasantries for a few minutes, and then he said, "Is Destiny there by any chance?"

Destiny and Vance were just walking in the house, and Althea said, "Colonel Thornton, please hold a moment. I hear her and Vance coming in now." Althea told Destiny, "Baby, you have a phone call."

Destiny asked, "Mama, who is on the phone for me?"

Althea explained, "It is Colonel Thornton."

Destiny hurried to the phone, and she said, "Hello, Colonel Thornton, how have you been?"

Colonel Thornton replied, "I have been well, Destiny, and I think I may have some good news for you. I made a few phone calls, and it would appear that the military police are in need of a Sergeant First Class MP; but Vance will not be able to accompany you when you go. He will report to Germany six months after you get there, for that is when his predecessor leaves."

Destiny was so happy she began to cry. She said, "Thank you, Colonel Thornton. I will tell Vance the good news." She then asked, "Colonel Thornton, are you coming down for the holiday with our family?"

Colonel Thornton said, "I wouldn't miss Thanksgiving with you and Althea. I look forward to seeing you all. Tell Vance hello for me."

With that exchange, Destiny and Colonel Thornton hung up.

Destiny went to the living room where Vance was sitting watching television.

Destiny said, "Vance, I have some good news and bad news. Which do you want first?"

Vance said, "Please give me the good news first."

Destiny said, "I just got off the phone with Colonel Thornton, and he informed me that there is a need for a SFC MP in Germany. The bad news is that you will not come over with me, but you will follow in six months."

Vance hugged and kissed Destiny after she gave him the news. Vance then said, "Let's call my parents and let them know the good news, after we tell Mrs. Drake."

They shared the good news with Althea, and she was happy for the both of them.

Later that evening, after his parents had arrived home from work, Vance called his father and said, "Dad, Destiny received a call from Colonel Thornton earlier this evening, and he informed her that there is a need for me in Germany." He also informed his father that he would be going over to Germany six months after Destiny had already been there.

Vance's father listened intently, and then he asked, "Son, you do still plan to ask Destiny to marry you, correct?"

Vance said, "I intend to speak with her mother while we are here, and then I will take it from there."

Two days later, Althea was in the kitchen cooking, when Vance walked in and sat at the counter. He asked, "Mrs. Drake, may I please talk to you about an important matter?"

Althea saw how serious Vance looked, so she said, "Sure you can, Vance" and sat down across from him. Althea asked, "Would you like something to drink?"

Vance said, "Yes, please." Althea retrieved two cokes from the fridge and two glasses from the cabinet. After they both were sipping their drinks and had gotten comfortable, Vance said, "Mrs. Drake, I am in love with Destiny. As you know, she is leaving going to Germany in less than three weeks. I would like to ask your permission to marry Destiny."

Althea sat for a moment, and then she looked Vance in the eyes and said, "Vance, Destiny is a grown woman. I am really honored that you would ask for my blessing in this matter, and I give you my blessing. The person whose permission you really need is Destiny's. By the way, are you planning to marry Destiny before she leaves for Germany? There is no way that we can plan a wedding in three weeks son."

Vance jumped off the kitchen stool and hugged Althea, kissing her on the cheek. He said, "Thank you so much for saying yes."

After dinner that evening, Vance asked Destiny to go for a walk with him. They walked down to the same spot by the brook as they did the first evening after he arrived. Vance and Destiny were standing watching the ducks play, and he got down on one knee and took Destiny's hand; then he said, "Destiny, will you marry me?" Destiny felt a tear slide down her face, because she was so shocked and happy at the same time. She looked at her finger and saw the one-carat diamond engagement ring that Vance had placed on her finger, and she mumbled, "Yes, Vance, I will marry you." Vance got up off his knees, lifted Destiny in his arms, and hugged and kissed her passionately. After that, they walked back to the house and shared their good news with Althea.

Destiny and Vance called his parents and shared the news of their engagement with them. His family was just as excited for the couple as Althea had been. There was one small detail that Vance forgot to mention to either of their parents. He was destined to marry Destiny before she left going to Germany. Vance was eager to return to Georgia, so that he could obtain a license and make Destiny his wife. He was certain that his commander would make a few calls and assist him in obtaining a license on such a short notice. Vance called his commander, Captain (CPT) Stuckey, and informed him of his engagement and his hopes to marry in less than three weeks.

Meanwhile, Colonel Thornton was happy that Destiny had found love after all that she had been through, but he was concerned as to why Vance wanted to marry before Destiny left. It was as if Vance had something to hide and he was hoping to marry Destiny before she found out. Colonel Thornton made a note to check into the matter, but then, he thought better of the notion. Maybe the young man was truly in love, and he was eager to have Destiny all to himself. Colonel Thornton would speak with Vance later about the matter.

Vance shared his idea with Destiny.

He explained his thought as such, "Destiny, I was thinking how great it would be if we were to get married before you left; that way, we would be guaranteed an opportunity to be stationed together, maybe sooner than the six months."

Destiny listened intently to Vance, voicing her fears, "Vance, we have less than three weeks before I fly to Germany; and that doesn't give us enough time to secure the paperwork, plan a wedding, and my get a name change applied for before I leave, not to mention we do the required military paperwork needed for military benefits and others."

Vance was disappointed that Destiny was so detail oriented, but he knew there was logic in what she said.

To the surprise of both Vance and Destiny, CPT Stuckey was able to secure the required paperwork. Colonel Thornton spoke with Vance and convinced him to have the ceremony at the court house and he would be there. Colonel Thornton also made a few calls to expedite the paperwork to ensure that Destiny would receive her name change and her benefits as married personnel and that she would be able to get quarters and such upon her arrival. With the details taken care of, Colonel Thornton had to ensure Althea was aware of the new plan and that she would be there for the ceremony.

Colonel Thornton called Althea and said, "Althea, how does your schedule look for the end of the week?"

Althea said, "My schedule is flexible, Michael. Why do you ask?"

Colonel Thornton went on to explain by saying, "Vance and Destiny have decided to get married before she leaves for Germany. I have taken the liberty to ensure their paperwork will be completed and the required documents will be available for Destiny to prove marriage before she leaves. Now, I would love to bring you down for the wedding; it will be at the court house here in Georgia. I thought it would be good if Destiny had both her mother and her protector at her side when she marries the man of her dream."

Althea said, "Colonel Thornton, I would not miss this moment for anything in the world. Destiny's happiness is important to me."

Colonel Thornton made reservations so that he could fly to Arkansas to escort Althea back for Destiny's wedding.

Destiny chose an ecru-colored dress that was knee length and fitted at the waist with tiny pleats had a slit in the back, and the neck-line was rounded with a slit forming a V in the center. Destiny wore a simple strand of pearls that she had been given by her aunt. The wedding party consisted of Vance's parents, Althea, Colonel Thornton, CPT Stuckey, and SSG Buckley. Vance and Destiny were married in the judge's chambers at Richmond County, in Augusta, Georgia.

Following the ceremony, Colonel Thornton had provided the couple with tickets to Hawaii for their honeymoon. Destiny hugged Colonel Thornton and thanked him for their tickets. She also hugged her new in-laws and thanked them for coming on such short notice.

Then she turned to Althea, and she saw that her mother had been crying.

Destiny said, "Mama, what is wrong? Why are you crying?"

Althea hugged her daughter and said, "Baby, these are tears of joy. My youngest child has married the man of her dreams; and that makes me so happy. Destiny, I think you chose well when you chose Vance."

Destiny hugged Althea tightly and said, "Thanks, Mama. That means a lot to me. Mama, do you think we should have waited to get married?"

Althea reassured Destiny by saying, "Destiny, Vance is so in love with you. He cannot stand the chance of losing you. All things happen in record time!"

Destiny and Vance left the courthouse and went to pack for their honeymoon.

Colonel Thornton walked over to Althea and said, "Althea, there is something strange about your new son, Vance, and I intend to get to the bottom of it."

Althea said, "Michael, I am glad that I am not the only one with that feeling. It would appear that my new son has something to hide; or why else would he be in such a hurry to marry Destiny? Michael, please keep me posted on what you find; I am curious about that young man."

Althea and Colonel Thornton went to the country club for lunch and to have a celebratory glass of wine.

Mr. and Mrs. Harmon left at ten o'clock in the evening on their honeymoon. Colonel Thornton gave them a lift to the airport. Vance was so excited to be married to Destiny. He could barely keep his hands off his new bride, and he was eager to consummate their marriage. Destiny on the other hand was having second thoughts about having married Vance so soon. She was wondering why Vance was in a hurry to get married. She knew he loved her deeply, but was that the only reason he married her so soon?

Colonel Thornton had spared no costs for this adventure for Destiny and Vance. Colonel Thornton had booked the newlyweds into the honeymoon suite at the *Moana Surfrider, A Westin Resort*

& Spa. There was a flute of champagne on ice for them when they arrived in their suite, and the *Do Not Disturb* sign was placed on the door by Vance. Vance and Destiny had a glass of champagne and ate some of the cake that was also a part of their gift. Vance wasted no time getting in the mood to celebrate their first night as Mr. and Mrs. Harmon.

Vance and Destiny made passionate love throughout the night. Destiny found that her new husband was a very skilled and attentive lover, making sure that his wife was totally satisfied before taking his own pleasure. Destiny and Vance spent the entire first day on bed, getting up only for food and bathroom breaks. They both lay in each other's arms totally satisfied and happily exhausted.

It was probably around midnight when Destiny got up to get herself a glass of water and she noticed an envelope that was slid under the door. It was a pink scented envelope, with Vance's name written on the back. The writing looked as if it had been written by a woman's hand, due to the neatness of the writing. Destiny picked up the envelope and took it back to the bedroom. Vance was lying on the bed waiting for Destiny to return. Destiny walked to the bed, handed the envelope to Vance, and asked, "Vance, what is going on? I found this envelope under the door when I went to get a glass of water a few minutes ago. Whom is this envelope from?"

Vance took the envelope from Destiny and patted the bed for her to come and sit beside him. Destiny did as he asked. Vance opened the envelope and removed the contents therein. There was a letter and a picture of a cute little boy who looked to be about two years old. He was a miniature version of Vance. Destiny saw the picture and began to tremble. She said, "Vance, is that your son?" Vance closed his eyes for a moment, and when he opened them, there were unshed tears in his eyes.

Vance took a deep breath and proceeded to tell Destiny a story: "About two years ago, I was stationed in Hawaii, and I met a girl at a party. We were all drinking and having a good time. I got drunk, and she and I ended up going back to her place. After I sobered up, we made love numerous times without any protection. She and I dated for a couple of months, and then she disappeared. Nine or so months later, she came to my unit with a newborn baby boy and told me he was my son. She just handed me the baby and walked away. I had a paternity test performed on the baby, and he was my son. I legally adopted my son per the instructions of the military legal advisor, and I asked my brother and his wife to care for him until I was married and able to care for him myself. Destiny, I was going to tell you this, but I was afraid you would not marry me if you knew I had a child. My parents said I should wait until we were married to tell you about Antonio Lamar Harmon, my two-year-old son."

Destiny stood up from the bed, walked to the dresser, looked at her watch, and dialed her new in-laws' number.

Destiny said in a very calm voice, "Hello, Mrs. Harmon, this is your new daughter Destiny, and I was just informed that I have a two-year-old stepson, Antonio. Were you aware of this information?"

Mrs. Harmon said, "Destiny, I thought it would be better if you were told after the wedding. This child has nothing to do with how Vance feels about you. He made a mistake, and now he has married you, a wonderful woman, who I think would make a wonderful mother."

Destiny informed Mrs. Harmon, "I would have liked to have been told in advance and been given an opportunity to choose whether or not I wanted a 'ready-made family.'"

Destiny hung up the phone, took a shower, got dressed, and asked Vance to take her to meet his son. Vance showered and dressed quickly, hailing a cab to his brother's home. Vance introduced Destiny to her new brother- and sister in-law.

Then Vance asked, "Where is Antonio?"

Daphne said, "He is sleeping."

As soon as Antonio heard his father's voice, he ran out the room and ran to Vance, screaming, "Daddy, you are back!"

Vance picked the child up and hugged and kissed him. Then Vance said, "Antonio, this is Destiny, my wife. She will be your new mother. Can you say hi?"

Antonio leaned over and hugged Destiny, and he said, "Hello, Mommy. I am glad you are going to be with me and my daddy."

Destiny hugged Antonio back, and she told him, "Antonio, thank you for letting me be a part of your and your daddy's life. I will try to be a good mom to you. It may take me some time to get things right, because being a mom is new to me. Will you help me get it right?"

Antonio nodded and reached for Destiny to take him, and she did, giving him a big hug and a kiss on his forehead.

Destiny and Vance left, with a promise to return the next day and take Antonio to the zoo. Destiny and Vance returned to their hotel room. Destiny was very quiet after returning to the room, using the time to process her thoughts. She smiled, because at that moment, it became clear why Colonel Thornton had given them tickets to Hawaii. Colonel Thornton wanted her to find out about her new husband's secret. Destiny knew there would be time for her to discuss that at a later date with her new "protector," Colonel Thornton.

Vance came into the sitting area where Destiny was curled up on the couch. He sat down on the couch and began to rub Destiny's feet. Then he continued up her legs and the length of her body, pulling Destiny into his lap and kissing her passionately.

Once he had finished kissing Destiny, he said, "Destiny, I am so sorry for keeping Antonio a secret. I wanted to make sure you loved me enough to give my son a home and the love he so desperately needs of a great mother like you."

Destiny laid her head on her husband's chest for a moment. Then she raised her head, wiped her eyes, and said, "Vance, don't ever keep secrets from me again. Are there any other surprises I am not aware of?"

Vance hugged her close and said, "No, sweetheart, that was my only secret. Destiny, I love you so much! Thank you for accepting my son." Vance made love to his wife that night with a clear conscience and the knowledge that Destiny loved both him and Antonio.

Destiny awoke to the sun shining in the window and the sound of laughter. Destiny showered and got dressed and then went out front to find her husband and stepson playing with a stuffed rabbit, monkey, and turtle. Destiny stood taking in the scene of father and son playing, and she knew that she had made the right choice.

Destiny walked over and said, "Good morning." Antonio squirmed out of Vance's arms, ran to Destiny, and hugged her leg. Destiny reached down and lifted him into her arms. Antonio hugged Destiny and said, "Good morning, Mommy." Those three words warmed Destiny's heart; she returned his hug, kissed his forehead, and held him close for a few moments.

Vance walked over and hugged Destiny while she held Antonio. Vance then kissed Destiny first and kissed his son on the top of his little head. Destiny, Antonio, and Vance left to get breakfast. They also bought bread from the store so that Antonio could feed the ducks, pigeons, and parrots at the zoo. The Harmon family then left going to enjoy their son and their day at the zoo.

Destiny and Vance took Antonio back over to Steve and Daphne, Vance's brother and sister in-law, after his trip to the zoo. Antonio fell asleep on Destiny's lap on the ride back home. Destiny kissed his forehead and hugged him closer to her. Vance was so proud of the love and attention his wife was showing to his son. Vance lifted Antonio from Destiny's lap and carried him in the house and put him to bed. Destiny gave Antonio a kiss before they left going back to the hotel.

CHAPTER 5

Revelation

Destiny and Vance said goodbye to their son, Antonio, with a promise to return for him soon. Destiny hugged Antonio, holding him close for a few minutes, as if she was remembering the way his little body felt. She kissed her son on the forehead and told him, "Mommy loves you so much. Please be good until I see you again." Destiny left the room with tears in her eyes. She was amazed at how quickly she had fallen in love with her new son.

Vance kissed Antonio with as much love as any father could show to his son, held him, and told him, "I love you, Antonio. Daddy will be back very soon; in the meantime (touching Antonio's pert nose with his forefinger), be a good boy for your aunt and uncle." The child smiled; hugged his daddy, laying his little head on his chest; and listened to his father's heartbeat.

Destiny and Vance returned to their hotel room, packed their suitcases, and prepared for their return trip to Fort Gordon, Georgia. Vance and Destiny were quiet on their ride to the airport, both having thoughts of their life when they returned to Georgia. Destiny was thinking that in less than two weeks' time, she would be leaving her husband just as she left her son, going to a foreign country to fight for freedom and justice and to make life better for their son. She knew that she would do whatever was required to maintain her career and protect her country, even if it meant breaking her own heart to do so.

Vance was thinking he had waited two years to find the woman whom he could love unconditionally, someone who would be a great mother to Antonio and a loving and devoted wife to him. Now that he had found Destiny, she was duty bound to her job, country, and way of life. He loved his wife, and he would miss her dearly, counting down the days until they were together again.

Their plane landed at the airport in Atlanta, and Colonel Thornton was waiting to give the newlyweds a ride to their apartment.

Colonel Thornton asked, "How was Hawaii? Destiny, did you enjoy your trip?"

Destiny smiled from the backseat and said, "I did. I enjoyed both my honeymoon and meeting my new son."

Colonel Thornton feigned surprise and said, "Your new son. What on earth are you talking about, Destiny?"

Destiny replied, "I met Antonio Lamar Harmon, Vance's two-year-old son."

Finally, Vance said, "Colonel Thornton, thank you for the tickets for our honeymoon and all that you have done to make my 'fairy tale' come true."

Colonel Thornton told Vance, "You are welcome. In the future, please make sure that there are no secrets between you and the one you love. Things could have gone differently, but I am glad everyone is happy with the present situation."

Vance mumbled, "Me too, and thanks for everything, sir."

Vance had now realized *honesty* would have been the best policy, but his biggest fear was losing Destiny once she found out about his son.

Colonel Thornton helped Vance secure their luggage and take it to their apartment. As Vance unlocked the door to their new home, he and Destiny were surprised by Althea, Stephanie, Mr. and Mrs. Harmon, and SSG Buckley. They were there to welcome Vance and Destiny home.

Althea and Mrs. Harmon had prepared dinner for the couple, and Mr. Harmon had provided the couple with a new stereo system and a forty-five-inch colored television. SSG Buckley gifted Destiny with a new lingerie set, informing Vance, "I think you will enjoy my gift to Destiny also, SFC Harmon." Destiny hugged Tiffany, trying to hold back the tears that were ready to fall.

Althea hugged both Destiny and Vance before she presented them with her gift. Althea presented Destiny and Vance with a check in the amount of two hundred thousand dollars.

She told them, "This is for the down payment on your first home, once you all return from Germany."

Destiny asked, "Mama, where did you get this money? I hope you didn't mortgage the house to give us this gift!"

Althea laughed and informed Destiny, "I have been waiting for the right moment to tell you this: When your father passed away, he made sure that I was well provided for. He left enough so that each of you four children would have an equal share as well. Your siblings received their portions when they married; now I am giving you your portion. Destiny, please accept this in the spirit that it is given. I love you, baby."

Everyone with the exception of Colonel Thornton was flabbergasted by Althea's gift to Vance and Destiny. Colonel Thornton smiled and hugged Althea, Destiny, and Vance. He then said, "Hey, everyone, the food is getting cold. Let's eat!" Everyone sat down at the table, and Mr. Harmon said grace; and everyone enjoyed the delicious meal that Althea and Mrs. Harmon had prepared.

Destiny cleared the table. She made a "to go" plate for Tiffany and Colonel Thornton. Then, Tiffany and Destiny washed, dried, and put away the dishes.

Once they were finished with the dishes, Tiffany asked, "How does it feel to be a married woman?"

Destiny smiled and said, "It feels fantastic. My only regret is Vance not being able to accompany me to Germany. I will savor every moment we have together before I leave!"

Tiffany hugged Destiny and told her, "God works in mysterious ways, Destiny. Just pray, and *he* will answer your prayers!"

Destiny knew there was logic in what Tiffany said, but right now her heart was hurting too much for her to see that logic.

Mr. and Mrs. Harmon excused themselves, with the excuse of having an early day for work. Colonel Thornton and Althea excused themselves as well. Colonel Thornton's excuse was he had to take Althea to the airport for her return trip home. And of course, Tiffany said, "It's time for me to go. You lovebirds need to catch up on your *private time together*. Make sure to wear my gift, Destiny."

Destiny and Vance saw their last guest off, and they were truly exhausted. Destiny took a long, luxurious bath in the bath salts that she had purchased in Hawaii and dabbed on a small amount of the perfume that Vance liked. She then waited for Vance to shower and come to bed.

Vance made passionate love to Destiny that night. He loved her as if his life depended upon it. Destiny shed tears of joy during their lovemaking, for she knew that Vance did not just love her body, but he loved her mind and soul as well. After their lovemaking session, long after Destiny was asleep, Vance held her in his arms, admiring each and every one of Destiny's features: from the slant of her nose to the curve of her hips. He had a mental picture of Destiny etched in his mind, so that he could recall it months after she was in Germany.

Vance awoke the next morning to the smell of bacon, eggs, grits, biscuits with sausage gravy, hash browns, and freshly squeezed orange juice. Vance showered and got dressed quickly, going to the kitchen. Vance entered the kitchen, and Destiny was at the stove finishing the hash browns. Vance walked up and hugged Destiny from behind, nuzzling her neck and planting a small kiss there.

He said, "Good morning, my love. You are up early."

Destiny explained, "I worked up an appetite last night, so I thought it would be nice for you to wake up to a good breakfast. After all, we have to keep your strength up." Then she giggled like a school girl.

Vance and Destiny ate their breakfast, did the morning dishes together, and decided to take a stroll around their new neighborhood. They walked hand in hand around the neighborhood, speaking to the neighbors that they met along the way. Then they stopped and checked their mail on the way back. Inside their mailbox was a letter from Daphne, and they were anxious to see what the letter said. Inside the envelope was a one-page letter, a picture that Antonio had drawn of three stick figures that represented Vance, Destiny, and

Antonio. There was also a picture of Antonio for both Vance and Destiny. Destiny was so happy to see Antonio's drawing; she hung it on their refrigerator and put his picture in her wallet.

Destiny and Vance were sitting watching television when the phone rang. Vance answered the phone, and it was Colonel Thornton. Colonel Thornton informed Vance that he needed to check in with his unit, because he had just received immediate orders to accompany his wife to Heidelberg, Germany.

Vance spent the next week and a half clearing the post, getting his belongings packed up (with Destiny's help) and shipped to Germany. He ensured that his passport was updated and that he had received the required vaccines to travel overseas to Germany. Both he and Destiny were ecstatic with the way things turned out. They knew that it was by the grace of God that this new turn of events happened. Destiny and Vance spent their final week in the guest house, waiting to fly out to Germany.

Colonel Thornton had a surprise of his own. He invited Vance and Destiny to dinner on Monday night to share his news with them. Colonel Thornton had received PCS orders to Darmstadt, Germany. He would report there after the first of the year. Destiny and Vance were excited, because Colonel Thornton would be in close proximity to them.

There was only one thing that hampered the excitement; SFC Jessup had requested retirement from the service. After twenty-two years of dedicated service, SFC Jessup was bidding the United States Army farewell. Destiny and Vance presented him with his retirement gift before they left for Germany. Destiny had researched each and every one of his duty assignments, she had compiled photos and gotten information from other soldiers he had been stationed with throughout his career, and she made a video of his life in the military. Not only did she produce the video, but she provided a voice narrating each and every detail of his service. Destiny presented the video and a diamond tie clip in the shape of an M16 bullet to SFC Jessup. These two gifts brought tears to his eyes. He hugged Destiny thanking her for both gifts.

Finally, the moment of truth arrived. Destiny and Vance bid goodbye to their family, and they boarded the plane to Germany. Destiny was one of the happiest women in the world. She was happy to have her husband with her in Germany. She was heartbroken that she was leaving her mother, but she knew Colonel Thornton would ensure Althea was okay while she was away. Destiny was grateful for the people in her life, especially Colonel Thornton, for he was like a father to her.

Thirteen hours later, Vance and Destiny arrived at their destination. They were weary and wanted nothing more than a hot shower and a bed. Unfortunately, they would not be able to enjoy either, for they spent another two hours in processing and meeting their commanders. Finally four hours after arriving in the country, Vance and Destiny were taken to eat and then to their temporary quarters. Destiny and Vance took a shower and went straight to bed. They fell asleep immediately.

Destiny awoke the next day to find that she had slept for twelve hours straight. Vance awoke after having slept ten hours. He showered, got dressed, and went to get them some food. Both Destiny and Vance were glad that they had three days to acclimatize before having to report for duty. Destiny showered and got dressed. After she and Vance had eaten, they explored their new surroundings to ensure they would be able to find their duty station from their present living quarters.

This was the couple's first time in Germany, so a lot of their morning was spent enjoying the beautiful environment, markets, and storekeeps and listening to the beautiful language as it was being spoken. Vance was so glad to be in the country with his wife. He and Destiny walked from store to store admiring the beautiful trinkets and clothes that were on display. Destiny fell in love with an adorable little jacket that she was sure would look handsome on Antonio. The jacket was made of Sherpa and had white fleece lining on the inside, on the collar, and around the cuffs. It was hand-stitched with beautiful embroidery on the left breast pocket; and she couldn't resist buying it for him.

Vance's heart sang with love. He didn't think it was possible to love anyone more than he already loved Destiny, but at that moment, his heart burst with love and gratitude for his wife. Vance hugged and kissed Destiny right there in the store, and several of the natives applauded and took pictures of the couple kissing. Destiny was swept off her feet by the kiss, and to be honest, she was a little embarrassed.

Little did Destiny know that the Germans were known for their public display of affection, and they found it very interesting to see Americans displaying their love and affection for one another. The three German men who were present invited Vance and Destiny to join them and their wives at the cantina to have a *Franziskaner Weissbier* (German beer made in Munich, Germany, from water, wheat malt, barley malt, yeast, and hop extract) with them. Destiny and Vance enjoyed their time with their newfound friends. These natives spoke English but with a heavy accent; and Destiny loved listening to them speak the language with their beautiful accent.

Vance and Destiny spent two hours at the cantina with their new friends, and then they left going back to their quarters. Destiny and Vance returned to their quarters, feeling great about their new assignment now that they had met some natives and made fast friends. Destiny reviewed the instructions for international calling, having purchased a calling card while they were out; she called Althea, her in-laws, and Colonel Thornton. Destiny let everyone know that they had arrived safely. After double-checking the time, she and Vance called their son, Antonio, and talked to him. Finally, they bid Antonio goodbye. Destiny had tears in her eyes by the time she hung up.

Vance assured Destiny, "As soon as it was feasible and the proper paperwork had been completed, I would return to Hawaii and bring our son home."

Destiny hugged Vance and informed him, "That is a promise that I intend to make sure you keep, husband of mine."

Despite the fact that it was only half past eight in the evening, Vance took the liberty to lure his wife to bed, with the intent of making sweet, passionate love to her. Destiny had no complaints with her husband's plans. As a matter of fact, she was disappointed that he had the idea first.

Destiny and Vance made passionate love off and on the entire night. Both were spent after their final session of lovemaking, and they held each other and drifted off to sleep, thinking of each other and how much he or she loved one another.

Destiny awoke to her phone ringing, and she slid from the bed making sure not to awaken Vance. Destiny retrieved the phone before it stopped ringing and whispered "Hello" into the phone. Destiny recognized Colonel Thornton's voice on her phone.

Colonel Thornton said, "Hello, Destiny, I received your message, and I wanted to call and hear your voice. How do you like Germany thus far?"

Destiny said, "Hello, Colonel Thornton, it is good to hear your voice. How are you doing? Have you heard from Mama since she went back home?" She informed him, "I am enjoying what I have seen so far. Vance and I had drinks with three couples yesterday, after they witnessed Vance kissing me in the store."

Colonel Thornton laughed, and then he explained, "One of the customs of German people is to publicly show their affection or love for each other. That means you and Vance are a big hit with the locals now. I did hear from Althea. She called and checked on me, since you guys are gone; she made sure I was okay. Destiny, I am so proud of the woman that you have become. Give my regards to Vance, and we will talk soon."

Destiny hung up the phone and joined her husband on the bed. This time, it was Destiny's idea to instigate their lovemaking. Vance was very much pleased with his wife's prowess in the bedroom; and he followed her lead, dancing to the song her body created.

After making love, both were starving. They crawled from bed, showered together, got dressed, and then made breakfast. Destiny made scrambled eggs, sausage, pancakes, and orange juice. Both devoured their meal and then cleaned the dishes. Once Destiny and Vance had finished the dishes and put them away, Destiny began working on their boots.

Destiny first polished her boots until they shined like glass, and then she made sure to buff and shine her husband's boots to the same luster. Vance removed first his uniform from the closet and pressed it until it would pass inspection; and he did the same to Destiny's uniform. Now that their uniforms were pressed and boots shined, they had more time to enjoy each other's company and explore the country.

That evening, Destiny and Vance walked down to the cantina and had dinner. They chose Jaegerschnitzel (fried breaded pork) with mushroom gravy, mashed potatoes, green beans with pork, and a hunk of thick crusty bread, all served with a glass of gluhwein or gluvine (hot mulled spiced wine served in Germany to chase off the winter chill). Destiny ate the entire serving of food that was on her plate and enjoyed the taste of the gluhwein. Both Destiny and Vance were stuffed and chose to forego dessert.

Destiny and Vance sat at the cantina and enjoyed the evening festivities that followed. The first entertainment consisted of the locals performing a traditional German folk dance—*Schuhplattler*—which consisted of leg, knee, and sole of the shoe slapping, performed to a ¾ beat, and yodeling. Once they were finished dancing, another group of individuals rose and enacted a story that depicted the German version of *Little Red Riding Hood*. Destiny's only regret was that Antonio was not there to see the wonder of storytelling, told by the German locals. Destiny and Vance took their leave and went home after the story was enacted.

The next day consisted of the couple resting, so that they would be ready to return to their duties. Destiny was excited about returning to work, especially since she had been informed by her commander of her new position. Unfortunately, Destiny's work ethic had preceded her, and she had returned to a position similar to the one she had left in Fort Gordon. Destiny would be in charge of the COMSEC facility; this time she would be responsible for maintaining secure communications for the entire military network in the country. She would travel from one base to the next to ensure they were able to communicate securely and effectively. Destiny looked forward to the challenge her new position would present.

Vance, on the other hand, was not looking forward to his new position. His new duties meant he would be stuck behind a desk all day, while his soldiers were out performing foot patrols, breaking up brawls, and totally enjoying their job as a military police. He was the senior personnel in charge of his station, and his job would consist of advising his troops on the necessary steps required to quiet a riot, stop the brawl without inciting more chaos and confusion, and things of that nature. Vance also realized that with this new position, there would be an added responsibility; he would be the individual reporting to the commander and taking the "butt chewings" from the commander when things did not go quite right. Vance thought things could be worse; had he followed his first mind when entering the service, he could have possibly been the commander.

The couple prepared to enjoy their last day together before returning to work. Destiny and Vance had a picnic in the park not far from their quarters, and they invited one of the local couples that they had drinks with earlier that week. All in all, their last day was relaxing and fun.

That night, Destiny and Vance did what most military personnel do when faced with a new position: They mentally prepared themselves for the upcoming day, showered, said their prayers, set the alarm clock, and went to sleep.

The next morning at precisely four o'clock, Destiny's alarm sounded. She immediately silenced the clock to prevent waking her husband. Destiny made breakfast and coffee, leaving the food to warm in the oven while she showered and readied herself for her first day of work. At the smell of food, Vance awoke before his alarm sounded, and he noticed that his wife was already dressed and waiting on him so that they could have breakfast. Vance showered quickly, got dressed, and went to the kitchen to have breakfast with Destiny. They ate breakfast, cleaned the dishes, and left for work.

Vance and Destiny walked outside to find the sky a beautiful blue, laced with a few fluffy clouds; but it was evident that the sun would shine, due to the purplish hue that was present as the clouds began to melt away. It was so beautiful that Destiny could not resist taking a photo of the sky as well as her surroundings as they walked to their company. Both Destiny and Vance walked to their perspective units, met with their sponsors, and began their in-processing procedures into their new brigade, battalion, and company. Destiny was ready to begin this new phase of her career.

CHAPTER 6

Investment

Destiny had overcome varied obstacles in her life and adjusted to her new role as wife and mother. But as Destiny would soon realize, everything in life happens for a reason. The people she encountered came into her life for a reason, a season, or a lifetime. Destiny must be ready to make decisions that would affect her life for years to come concerning some of these persons; and these decisions might require sacrifices in order to gain investments in her marriage, career, and life.

Destiny took inventory of the last eight months of her life; and she found that she was pleased with the results. In the last eight months, she had married a wonderful man, inherited a beautiful son, moved to a foreign country that she loved, and had a great job. Destiny came to the conclusion that she was truly blessed to have accomplished these goals thus far.

Despite her accomplishments, Destiny was still worried about her career as well as her family life. The last few weeks she had been extremely tired, regardless of the amount of rest and sleep she got. Not only had she been extremely tired, but she seemed to have caught some type of virus, because her stomach had been upset and she had had several bouts of nausea lately. Destiny also noticed that her normal clothes were getting a little snug in the hips and the waistline.

Destiny awoke the next morning and was fixing breakfast for her and Vance when she immediately felt dizzy and had an upset stomach. Destiny turned off the sausage that she was cooking and rushed to the bathroom to empty the contents of her stomach. Vance was heading to the kitchen from their bedroom when he heard Destiny retching in the bathroom. Vance knocked on the door and asked, "Destiny, are you okay in there?" As the question left his lips, poor Destiny was experiencing another bout of vomiting. Vance became alarmed and informed Destiny, "Babe, I think we should get you to the doctor and see if she can give you something to settle your stomach." Destiny was too weak to argue; she cleaned herself up, got her coat, and allowed Vance to escort her to the doctor.

Vance took Destiny to the clinic, and she was seen by the on-call doctor, Dr. Woodburn, a beautiful woman in her mid-forties, glasses, and a patient demeanor.

Dr. Woodburn asked Destiny, "Mrs. Harmon, what brings you in today?"

Destiny explained her symptoms by saying, "I have been totally exhausted for the last couple or so weeks. I am always sleepy and have had nausea and an upset stomach for the last couple weeks, and I almost passed out this morning while preparing breakfast."

Dr. Woodburn said, "I see. Mrs. Harmon, are you experiencing nausea and vomiting only during the mornings or throughout the day?"

Destiny answered, "I mostly experience the nausea and vomiting during the mornings, but when I smell certain foods being cooked, it happens then also."

Dr. Woodburn asked Destiny to provide a urine sample; and she also performed a blood test on Destiny. Since it was still morning, Dr. Woodburn tested her theory. She presented Destiny with a cup of ginger ale and said, "Mrs. Harmon, would you please drink this seltzer, wait fifteen minutes, and tell me how your stomach feels?" Destiny did as she had been asked, and after the allotted time, she found that her stomach was no longer queasy and she felt better.

Thirty minutes later, Dr. Woodburn walked in the examination room with Vance in tow. She instructed Vance, "Mr. Harmon, please have a seat with Mrs. Harmon."

Vance did as he was told. Vance asked, "Doctor, will my wife be okay?"

Dr. Woodburn smiled and replied, "Mr. and Mrs. Harmon, congratulations! Mrs. Harmon is eight weeks pregnant." Destiny passed out upon hearing the news. Dr. Woodburn used smelling salts and brought Destiny out of her "faint." Dr. Woodburn informed Destiny, "I am writing a profile for you to be on light duty only, no stressful situations for the next eight or so weeks. I would like to see you back in my office in four weeks." Dr. Woodburn presented Destiny and Vance with some literature on pregnancy, presented Destiny with a prescription for prenatal vitamins and iron supplements, and sent them on their way.

Destiny was still in shock after finding out that she was pregnant. She looked at Vance, and he was smiling from ear to ear.

Vance said, "Babe, can you believe it? Antonio is going to be a big brother! I am so excited that we are having a baby."

Destiny sat there, letting the news sink in. Destiny said to Vance, "Please stop by the pharmacy so that I can fill these prescriptions." Destiny was thinking about how her being pregnant would ultimately change everything for her. Hell, it would change her life completely!

Destiny was thinking, *Well, why wouldn't Vance be happy? After all, he just has to wait seven more months, while I grow fat, cranky, and tired. My feet would be swollen, and I would be a total mess. How in the hell did I let this happen? Why didn't I use protection during my first couple months of marriage? What about my career? How could I manage a baby and a toddler at the same time while juggling my career?* Destiny filled her prescriptions, left the pharmacy, got in the car, and rode home with her husband.

Destiny and Vance had just walked in their home from the clinic when the phone rang. It was one of Vance's soldiers calling to inform him of an incident that was taking place on post. Vance informed Destiny, "Babe, there is a problem with work; I have to report to the office. I will call you if I am going to be late for dinner." Destiny nodded, and Vance was out the door.

Destiny sat on the couch, and the next thing she knew, Vance was shaking her to wake her up.

Destiny asked, "How long have you been home?"

Vance explained, "I came home and found you asleep on the couch; then I left to go pick up dinner from the cantina. How are you feeling?"

Destiny sat up on the couch and said, "I am feeling much better after having taken a nap."

Vance smiled and kissed Destiny, wrapping his arms around her and lifting her from the couch and carrying her to the table so that they could eat dinner.

Destiny enjoyed the schnitzel with hunter's gravy, noodles, salad, and crusty bread. After eating their dinner, Vance and Destiny snuggled up on the couch and reviewed the literature that they had been given by Dr. Woodburn. Destiny noticed that in one of the pamphlets that she was reading, it was written "the mother-to-be may experience having to urinate frequently, due to the baby sitting on the mother's bladder." Destiny thought, *Just great! This is great, something else for me to look forward to during this pregnancy.*

Vance hugged Destiny tight and said, "Destiny, I don't think our getting pregnant could have happened at a better time, do you?"

Destiny replied, "Vance, I beg to differ with you. The one thing that you fail to understand is how my being pregnant will affect everything concerning me! Of course, you would be happy. You are not the one who will be gaining weight and having your stomach stretched beyond its normal capacity; nor will you have to worry about going to pee every fifteen minutes as the baby grows bigger!"

Vance looked at Destiny with hurt in his eyes and said, "Destiny, if you were so worried about not wanting to have my baby, maybe you shouldn't have made love to me without birth control." He walked out of the quarters and slammed the door behind him.

Destiny felt a little awkward, because she had just instigated their first ever argument during their marriage. Destiny felt bad that she had upset Vance, but she also knew she was telling the truth; and she would not apologize for ever telling the truth! At that moment, Destiny remembered her religious teachings and realized that her pregnancy was a gift, one that she should be happy about; instead here she was being selfish and thinking only of herself. Destiny felt ashamed of her behavior concerning her innocent, unborn child, and for the first time, she began to realize this pregnancy was a "gift from God"; and she would cherish the gift that she had been given, instead of being selfish and ungrateful.

When Vance returned home an hour later, Destiny was sitting on the couch reading more of the pamphlets that she had received earlier that day.

Vance walked over to the couch and sat down by his wife, and he said, "Destiny, I am sorry for my behavior. It's just that you don't seem to be happy about 'our' pregnancy."

Destiny took her husband's hand in hers and looked him in his eyes and said, "Vance, I am sorry too. It's just that I was scared when I thought about my being pregnant and how it would change our lives forever. I was wrong to voice my fears out loud and make you feel bad about your being happy about the pregnancy."

Vance hugged and kissed Destiny, telling her, "This is *our* baby whom you are carrying, and I love you. I realized how scared you must be right now, but, baby, I will be right here with you; and we will go through this pregnancy together!"

Destiny felt so relieved to know that her husband understood her fears and was willing to make the required sacrifices together.

Time seemed to fly by. Before Destiny realized it, her four weeks were up, and she was at her appointment with Dr. Woodburn. Dr. Woodburn informed Destiny and Vance that "the purpose of today's visit was for her to check the baby's heartbeat and make sure the baby was healthy and growing properly." Dr. Woodburn had Destiny lie on the bed; she put her stethoscope on Destiny's stomach and listened intently for a heartbeat. Dr. Woodburn smiled, and she moved the stethoscope around twice to make sure she was hearing what she heard. Dr. Woodburn said, "Mr. and Mrs. Harmon, I hear a very strong heartbeat, but I would also like to perform an ultrasound today just to make sure everything is progressing normally." She then allowed both Destiny and Vance to hear the baby's heartbeat; at that very moment, they both fell in love with their unborn child.

Finally the holidays arrived, and Destiny was showing. It was then that she called Althea and her in-laws and shared the news. Althea was so happy she began to cry saying, "Destiny, I am so proud of you and Vance, and I know you will be a great mom. Give my love to Vance." Destiny then called her in-laws and shared the news of their pregnancy with them. Destiny's in-laws were totally excited, because now they would have two grandchildren to spoil. They could not wait until the baby was born.

Mrs. Harmon asked, "Do you all know the sex of the baby yet?"

Destiny explained, "Vance and I want it to be a surprise to everyone, us included."

Mrs. Harmon was so proud of her son and daughter, and she wasted no time letting them both know it.

Christmas was a joyous time for Vance and Destiny. First, Althea flew over one week before Christmas; and then Colonel Thornton came over three days later. Colonel Thornton was so surprised when he saw Destiny pregnant.

He joked, "Destiny, did you swallow a watermelon or something?"

Destiny smiled and said, "No, I am just seven months pregnant with your first God child."

Just at that moment, the baby decided to give a swift kick, and Destiny allowed Colonel Thornton to place his hand on her stomach and feel the baby's second kick. This small gesture brought tears to Colonel Thornton's eyes, and he hugged both Vance and Destiny at the same time to prevent them from seeing his tears of joy for them and the fact that he had missed this opportunity in his life.

Little did Destiny know that Vance had asked Althea to remain in Germany until the baby was born; and she had agreed to spend the next four or so months there with them. Colonel Thornton would be taking his leave there as well, since he would be reporting to his new duty station after the New Year.

Colonel Thornton had made reservations to stay at the guest house there on post, but Vance would not hear of it.

He explained, "Colonel Thornton, our quarters has three bedrooms, and that means you and Mama Althea will be staying here with us while you are here."

Colonel Thornton said, "Thank you, Vance. That means a lot to me."

Destiny and Vance shared the same tradition that they both grew up with; the family arose early on Christmas morning and opened their gifts. Vance gifted Destiny with a beautiful mother's ring that had her birthstone, Antonio's birthstone, and a stone for February, the month that their new baby would be born. He also purchased tiny new clothes for their baby as well as a bassinette. These items brought tears to Destiny's eyes, and she hugged Vance with their baby kicking them both. Vance and Destiny laughed, and Vance said, "Hey, little one, behave. We love you very much," as he rubbed his wife's belly.

Destiny gave Vance a new Rolex watch that he had been admiring since they had been in the country. Vance was so shocked when he opened the box and saw the watch; he hugged his wife, lifting both her and the baby off the floor twirling them around. Vance kissed his wife and said, "Thank you, babe." The second gift that Destiny gave Vance was a poem that she had written and framed. The poem was a token of her love to Vance, and she thanked him for being her husband and the father of her two children. This gift brought tears to Vance's eyes, and he had to compose himself after reading it. Vance passed the poem to Althea and Colonel Thornton for their review.

Colonel Thornton and Althea gave the couple security bonds in the amount of one thousand dollars each. There were a total of eight security bonds, two for Antonio, two for the new baby, and two for each of Destiny and Vance. Destiny could no longer hold back the tears that fell; she was so blessed to have Colonel Thornton, Althea, and her husband in her life.

Destiny gave Althea a diamond necklace with a matching bracelet that she and Vance had both purchased and had engraved *We will always love you.* Destiny presented Colonel Thornton with two gifts: One was a beautiful set of golf clubs engraved with his initials, *M.*

T., since he always wanted to learn to play golf; and the second was a medium-sized gift box with a framed picture of Destiny, Althea, SFC Jessup, and Colonel Thornton. There was a pink envelope inside the box. It contained a note to Colonel Thornton saying, *Thank you for being a father figure to me, a protector, and a true friend. Love, Destiny.* Now it was Colonel Thornton's turn to shed some tears, and he hugged Destiny and kissed her on the top of her head. He showed the letter to Althea, and she had tears in her eyes after reading the note.

Christmas Day was a joyous occasion; Althea and Destiny were in the kitchen cooking, while Colonel Thornton and Vance were watching the games and sneaking food when the ladies weren't watching. Althea made a huge glazed ham, candied yams with marshmallows, green beans with chopped potatoes, corn on the cob, roast beef with mushroom gravy, rice, and a huge salad. For dessert, Althea baked two sweet potato pies, a German chocolate cake, and two pecan pies. She also made eggnog with and without liquor, ensuring Destiny drank the one without liquor. Destiny especially enjoyed the glazed ham, and she and the baby ate two helpings of it.

Colonel Thornton laughed and teased Destiny saying, "Destiny, we are going to have to use a wheel barrow to get you and that baby in the car."

Destiny smiled and said, "We are enjoying our dinner, so get the wheel barrow ready."

Everyone laughed.

After dinner, Vance, Destiny, Colonel Thornton, and Althea all went for a walk, to walk off some of the dinner they had overindulged on.

Vance asked Destiny, "Destiny, do you feel up to walking to the cantina?" Destiny said "Sure." She thought Althea and Colonel Thornton would enjoy the locals' festivities. The owner of the cantina hadn't seen Destiny since she had begun to show, and when she saw Destiny, she was so happy and hugged her and then rubbed her big belly. Destiny introduced Althea and Colonel Thornton, and the lady said, "I see where you get your beauty, Frau Destiny; it is from both Mom and Dad!" Neither Althea nor Colonel Thornton had the heart to correct her. Destiny smiled and introduced them both as simply her "mom and dad." This made Colonel Thornton stand a little taller than his six-feet-and-two-inch height.

Frau Tilderchaun served gluvine to Althea, Vance, and Colonel Thornton, giving Destiny warmed apple cider with a cinnamon stick. Everyone drank their beverage and enjoyed the festivities. Once the dancing and storytelling was over, Frau T. had her husband give Destiny and Althea a ride, while Vance and Colonel Thornton chose to walk back, so that they could talk.

Colonel Thornton asked Vance, "What are your plans concerning Antonio?"

Vance explained, "I plan to go get him sometime after the New Year, giving him time to get used to Mama Althea and the idea of Destiny having a baby."

Colonel Thornton said, "I think that is a good idea. This way he will better understand about the baby. I think it will do Destiny some good as well, because she will get used to having a 'small person' in the house."

Vance went on to explain to Colonel Thornton that he had put in for two months' leave, so that he could spend time with his family and helping out with the baby and Antonio. Colonel Thornton had to admit he was proud of Vance and the choices he was making. Maybe Vance would be a great father. So far he was proving to be a good husband to Destiny.

Destiny and Vance were loving having Althea there. Each morning before they left going to work, Althea had a hot breakfast ready for them. She would also prepare lunch and have it ready when they came in at noon, and supper was ready for them when they arrived home promptly at five o'clock.

Vance said, "Mama Althea, I am going to gain so much weight with all your good cooking, but I will just have to run an extra mile or so."

Althea laughed and said, "Thanks, son."

It was January 3, 1993; and Vance was leaving Germany, flying to Hawaii to bring their son, Antonio, home. Althea was so excited to meet her newest grandchild, and she had purchased Antonio a big teddy bear and a Tonka truck to play with. Althea and Destiny had taken the time to set up both Antonio's room and the bassinette for the baby. Althea took the liberty to wash and fold all the baby clothes to ensure they would be ready when the time came. While Vance was gone, Althea made sure she and Destiny continued to complete their daily walks, so that Destiny would have an easier labor and childbirth.

One week after Vance had flown to Hawaii, Destiny took off from work, so that she and Althea could both welcome Antonio home. Althea had taken the liberty of baking a cake that said, *Welcome home, Antonio*, and when Destiny heard Vance's key in the door, she was totally excited. She stood there with her arms open wide waiting to hug her new son. Antonio started to run toward Destiny, but he stopped when he saw her protruding belly; and he walked the rest of the way.

He hugged his new mom and said, "Mommy, I missed you so much!" Then he touched Destiny's stomach and said, "Baby."

Destiny said, "Yes, we are having a baby, Antonio; and you will be a big brother."

Althea picked Antonio up and hugged him ever so close and said, "Hello, Antonio, I am Granny Althea, and I am so pleased to see you."

Antonio hugged Althea and said, "Hi, Granny, how are you?"

Althea kissed him on his forehead and laughed, walking into the kitchen with him still in her arms. She asked Vance, "Is it okay if he cuts his cake and eats a slice?"

Vance was so overjoyed at the reception Althea gave his son he could only nod his head yes, with tears in his eyes. Destiny hugged and kissed her husband saying, "Thank you for keeping your promise to me. I love you." Vance kissed his wife long and deep and put his arm around her waist, and they walked in the kitchen for cake and ice cream.

Althea gave Antonio the first piece of cake; and then she served Vance, Destiny, and herself.

They enjoyed the cake and ice cream, and then Antonio hugged Althea and said, "Thank you, Granny, for the cake."

Althea hugged him back and said, "You are welcome, baby."

Vance was just so happy that his son was getting along so well with his new granny. Althea read Antonio a story, and then they played with the toys in his room. Antonio began to yawn, and Althea put him down for a nap, and then she started dinner.

In honor of her new grandson, Althea made chicken strips, French fries, and green beans for dinner. For dessert, she made vanilla pudding cups and sat them in the refrigerator.

Vance said, "Wow, Mama Althea, why don't I get this type of special treatment?"

Althea hugged him and said, "You are my son, not my grandson. That is why."

Vance smiled and hugged Althea again saying, "Thank you for loving our son."

Althea said, "He is my grandson, and I wouldn't have it any other way!"

Antonio woke up and asked, "Where is my granny?"

Althea heard him from the kitchen and said, "Granny is in the kitchen setting the table; you can come help me please." Antonio ran to the kitchen to help his granny. Once Antonio and Althea were finished setting the table, they said in unison, "Dinner is ready!" Vance and Destiny laughed and walked to have dinner.

January quickly came to a close, and Destiny and Althea were enjoying having Antonio there, and Vance was just ecstatic that things were going so well. February roared in like a lion with crisp weather, and everyone was staying inside. It was the 13th of February, at ten o'clock in the evening, when Destiny's water broke. Unfortunately, she had been in labor most of the day but was not aware of it. Althea helped Destiny get redressed, handed Vance the suitcase and car keys, and called ahead alerting the hospital that Destiny's water had broken fifteen minutes ago and they were on their way to the hospital. Althea kept Antonio, and they were sitting at home awaiting the news of the delivery.

At two in the morning on February 14, 1993, Destiny welcomed their daughter, Briana Chane Harmon. Briana weighed eight pounds and three ounces and was twenty-one inches long. She had beautiful brown eyes like her mother and a head full of black, curly hair like her father. Vance was so excited to cut the umbilical cord and be the very first person to hold his daughter. He was the happiest man in the world at that very moment. He then checked on his wife and gave the baby to Destiny so she could have a glimpse at their beautiful baby girl.

Colonel Thornton was out in the waiting room, walking a hole in the carpet, awaiting news of his God child and Destiny. After Destiny had been cleaned up and moved into a room, the baby was cleaned, dressed, and placed in an incubator in the room beside her mother's bed. Colonel Thornton was escorted in by the nurse to see Destiny and Briana. Destiny was sitting up on the bed.

Colonel Thornton walked in and hugged her saying, "I am so proud of you. You are one of the bravest people I know, Destiny Harmon. Thank you for allowing me to be here for this very special moment."

Destiny smiled and said, "Michael, you are family, and we would not have it any other way. Please take your God daughter and say hello to her."

Colonel Thornton held the baby ever so gingerly and rocked her until she dozed off to sleep.

Vance handed out cigars to everyone he met, and he was so proud to have Destiny as his wife and the mother of his children. Destiny and Vance called Althea and Antonio and told them the good news. Once they had hung up with Althea and Antonio, Vance called his parents to share the news. By this time, Destiny and the baby had both drifted off to sleep, and Vance sat by the bed holding Destiny's hand. He placed a kiss upon Destiny's brow while she slept and uttered, "Destiny, thank you for our daughter. I love you with all my heart!"

Three days later, Destiny and Briana were released to go home. Colonel Thornton and Althea had balloons in the living room along with a beautiful pink banner that said, *Welcome home, Destiny and Briana. We love you!* Destiny handed Briana to Althea, and she bent down to hug and kiss her son telling him, "Mommy missed you so much, and I would like for you to come say hello to your little sister, Briana." Antonio hugged his mom and walked with her to see his new baby sister. Vance stood and watched as his wife introduced their son to their new addition to the family. Antonio kissed his little sister on the cheek. Althea and Colonel Thornton were elated with what they witnessed.

As the weeks flew by, Destiny noticed that her daughter was gaining her own personality. She was gaining weight, and she recognized her big brother. Destiny breastfed Briana, and it seemed to Destiny this child was always hungry. On the other hand, Destiny noticed that she was losing weight and was able to get back into some of her clothes that she wore before getting pregnant. Destiny looked in the mirror and admired how quickly her body was transforming after childbirth. Her stomach was almost back to normal. Her hips were slightly wider, and her breast size increased from a 36C to a 42C. Vance truly loved his wife's new curves, and he was counting the weeks until he could explore those curves once again.

Destiny was enjoying motherhood, spending time with her son and daughter. Destiny and Antonio would play hide and seek when Briana was asleep, and she would spend time cuddling with her son and reading him stories. Destiny was teaching Antonio his alphabets and how to write his numbers from one to twenty. Destiny was a firm but patient mom, knowing when to scold and when a hug was in order. Althea was proud of her daughter and her mothering techniques.

Althea was spending time equally with her grandchildren and enjoyed time with Destiny as well. The entire family was having a joyous time together. Briana was growing into a beautiful five-month-old baby. She had big beautiful brown eyes, rosy cheeks, and ringlets of curls that bounced when she kicked her little legs and feet. Vance was really happy to be able to spend time with his son and watch his daughter grow.

Colonel Thornton came to visit and brought Antonio a football. He and Vance went outside and played football with Antonio so that he could see how things were going.

Antonio tackled Colonel Thornton and said, "Daddy, I tackled Papa. Look. I got the ball."

Colonel Thornton gave Antonio a great big bear hug and said, "Yes, you did tackle Papa, and that means you won." After that, Colonel Thornton asked Vance, "Is it okay if I treat Antonio to an ice-cream cone? You are welcome to come have one with us."

Vance nodded, and they went for ice cream and a movie. It was boys' day out, and the three of them had a glorious time together.

Michael Thornton would never have thought that his meeting a slip of a soldier like Destiny could lead to this much happiness. He told Vance as much on their ride home, and he also thanked Vance for allowing him to be a part of his family. Michael explained, "I was so focused on my career that I forgot to have fun. I didn't have time to date much, and the truth was there weren't many women whom I was attracted to. As I progressed through the ranks, the females whom I could date became limited to me, and I never had time to explore the civilian females. I dated this female for about six months. I thought we were doing okay, but then she sent me a 'Dear John' letter because I wasn't there enough. I am so glad that you didn't make the same mistake in that area as I did, Vance, and I thank you for taking care of Destiny. Destiny is like a daughter to me, and ever since she was hurt in Korea, I have been overprotective of her. That was so long ago. The only other woman that I have cared for has been Althea, but I would never embarrass either of us by making it known. Althea and Destiny have become my family over the years."

Vance was so happy he had spent the day with Michael Thornton, because he had gotten to see a side of him he otherwise would never have known. Vance said, "I am sorry that you never found love in your younger years, but it is never too late to express that love now to Althea. I think that deep down she feels the same way about you that you feel about her. Both Destiny and I are okay with it, if you two do decide to explore a relationship. Michael, life is too short to not enjoy it when you have the opportunity to do so."

CHAPTER 7

Reverie

Destiny tossed and turned most of the night; and at about three o'clock, she got out of bed to go check on her children, Antonio and Briana. Antonio was fast asleep with his favorite stuffed animal clenched in his left hand; and Briana was fast asleep in her crib with her thumb in her mouth. Destiny kissed both children on their foreheads, pulled the covers over them snugly, and went to get herself a glass of water.

She stood in the kitchen and sipped her glass of water, thinking about the dream that had awakened her. She decided she would wait a couple of hours before calling Althea to check on her, so she went back to her bedroom and slowly crawled back on bed, trying not to awaken Vance. Once she had laid down, Vance put his arm around her and pulled her close; and that was the last thing that Destiny remembered, for she fell fast asleep in her husband's embrace.

Destiny awoke to Briana crying, and she got up to go check on her. She picked Briana up from her crib and held her close, and then she understood why she was crying. Destiny and Briana headed straight to the bathroom, and Destiny turned on the water in the bathtub, took care of Briana's diaper, and then gave the baby a bath.

Destiny dressed Briana in another sleeper outfit and played with her. After Destiny had taken care of Briana, she left Briana with Vance, got a shower, and started breakfast for her family. She made pancakes, eggs, sausage, hash browns, and some bacon. She then squeezed fresh orange juice for Vance, Antonio, and herself. She called from the kitchen, "Brunch is ready," and the entire crew came running, with Vance leading them all. Destiny smiled, took Briana from Vance's arms, placed her in her high chair, and prepared food for her. Destiny then fixed Antonio's plate and sat it in front of him. Antonio waited until his mom and dad fixed their plates, came to the table, and said grace; and they all began to eat.

Vance cleaned the dishes and the kitchen, while Destiny assisted Antonio in taking a bath. Once he was dried off and after putting his body lotion, Destiny assisted her son in getting dressed. Destiny and Vance had promised Antonio a trip to the zoo, and he could hardly wait for everyone to get dressed so that they could leave. Destiny dressed Briana and herself and waited for Vance to ready himself as well. Finally, the Harmons were off to the zoo for a day of fun, laughter, and excitement!

Briana enjoyed the outing as much as her big brother. They both watched the animals in amazement and were in awe when the parrots began to talk. Vance and Destiny took the children to eat after the zoo, and then Antonio wanted to go to the park.

Destiny said, "Antonio, you can go to the park after you and Briana take a nap. It has been a long day, and both you and your sister are overdue for a nap."

Antonio knew that his mom was right, so he said, "Okay, Mommy."

Destiny and Vance arrived home, and both Antonio and Briana were put down for their nap. As soon as their heads hit their pillows, the children were fast asleep. Vance and Destiny used the time to relax and enjoy each other's company, since they seldom got any time alone these days with a baby and a toddler in the house. They discussed the possibility of going home to visit Vance's parents, since they had not had an opportunity to meet their granddaughter yet.

Destiny and Vance were cuddled up on the couch when the phone rang, and Vance answered it since he was closer to it. It was Colonel Michael Thornton on the line, asking whether or not it would be feasible for him to come down and visit the babies on the upcoming weekend.

Vance assured him, "It would be great for you to come visit. Antonio is asking when Papa is coming back."

Colonel Thornton asked, "Is my grandson available for me to speak to?"

Just about that time, Antonio was walking in the room from his nap. Vance beckoned Antonio over saying, "Papa is on the phone, and he wants to speak to you."

Antonio told Colonel Thornton all about his trip to the zoo and all the animals that he saw. Antonio asked, "Papa, when are you coming over to see me and Briana?"

Colonel Thornton said, "I will be down this weekend to see you and Briana. Maybe you and I can play football and some more games that you like."

Antonio said, "Okay, Papa, I love you."

Those three words warmed Colonel Thornton's heart, and he said, "I love you too, Antonio. Give Briana a kiss for me."

Colonel Thornton spoke to Vance and Destiny, and then he signed off. Destiny checked on Briana, who was still sleeping; and then she went to start dinner. Destiny chose to make a simple dinner for the family; she made a salad, baked chicken, and made corn on the cob, mashed potatoes, and sweet tea. After everyone had eaten their dinner and the kitchen was cleaned and dishes washed and put away, Destiny and Vance took the children to the park to run off dinner and have a good time.

Forty minutes later, the Harmon family returned home to find their phone ringing as they were walking in the door. It was Althea. Althea sounded as though she had been crying.

Destiny asked, "Mama, what is wrong? You sound like you are crying."

Althea then explained, "Destiny, please sit down if you are not already seated. I called to inform you that your nephew has been in an accident."

Destiny was worried and began to tremble. She asked, "Mama, which of the boys was in the accident?"

Althea told her, "It was Marcellus. He was riding his motorcycle, and he was hit from behind by a drunk driver. The impact caused him to lose control of the bike he was thrown from it; and he was hit by an oncoming eighteen-wheeler, and he died instantly."

Destiny sat there, unable to speak for a moment, and Vance came and took the phone. Vance asked Althea, "Mama, are you okay? When is the funeral?"

Althea said, "I was calling to see if you and Destiny were going to come home for the funeral. If you all are planning to come home, we can push the date back." Vance looked at Destiny and she nodded yes. Vance affirmed that they would be home for the funeral.

Destiny sat on the couch and cried as her husband held her. After all her tears were spent, she turned to Vance and said, "Vance, I was awakened at three this morning by a bad dream. In my dream I kept seeing you falling down the stairs, and I was not able to get to you in time. I didn't know what the dream meant at the time, but I couldn't get it out of my mind. Now I know what it meant."

Vance said, "Destiny, what are you talking about?"

"Vance, ever since I can remember, I would have nightmares or get a bad feeling just before something bad would happen to someone I cared about. It first happened when my father was killed. I woke up screaming because I had seen Daddy in a car accident and he was not moving."

Vance pulled Destiny close and said, "Baby, I am so sorry that you had to experience that trauma, but anytime you have any more dreams, please talk to me about them, okay?"

Destiny nodded okay and continued to lay her head on her husband's chest.

Destiny called Colonel Thornton to inform him that they would have to cancel the visit this weekend. She explained, "Mama called me a short while ago to inform me that Marcellus, my nephew, was killed in a motorcycle accident. Vance, the children, and I are going home for the funeral. We will put in for leave tomorrow and try to leave as quickly as possible."

Colonel Thornton asked, "How is Althea? Would you mind if I attended the funeral? I think Althea might need some support to get through this ordeal."

Destiny said, "I think Mama would like that Michael, and so would I."

The next day, Destiny and Vance put in for three weeks' leave to go home for Marcellus's funeral. The plan was to spend a couple of days with Vance's parents while they were home, so that they could see their grandchildren, especially Briana. Two days later, the Harmon family left Germany going to Arkansas for the funeral. The Harmons arrived in Little Rock, and Althea was waiting at the airport to greet them. Althea was surprised at how much her grandbabies had grown. Antonio saw his granny, and he ran and hugged Althea's leg. Althea picked Antonio up, hugged him, and kissed his forehead.

She asked, "How is granny's young man doing?"

Antonio said, "I am good now, Granny. I am with you."

That brought tears to Althea's eyes; she hugged him again, this time holding him for a moment longer. Althea hugged Destiny and Vance one-arm style since she was still holding Antonio in the other. Althea kissed her son and daughter, as well as Briana. Vance secured the luggage and stored it in the car. Althea gave Vance the car keys so that he could drive while she visited with both her grandbabies.

Vance was driving from the airport and Althea was sitting between Briana and Antonio playing with them both when Destiny's phone rang. It was Colonel Thornton.

He informed Destiny, "I just arrived at the airport here in Little Rock. I have a rental car, and I am driving down to Althea's house."

Destiny said, "Hold on, Michael. We are just leaving the terminal. We are returning to the terminal to meet you."

Michael said, "Is Althea with you all?"

Destiny said, "Yes, she is."

Michael asked, "May I speak with Althea, please?"

Destiny handed the phone to her mother and said, "Mama, it's Michael. He wants to speak to you."

Althea took the phone and said, "Hello, Michael, how have you been?"

Michael replied, "I have been well, Althea. I hope it is okay I came here to be your support system for your grandson's funeral."

Althea said, "Michael, that means so much to me. Thank you for being so thoughtful."

The Harmon family and Althea returned to the airport, and they saw Michael standing at the rental car desk. Antonio ran over, and Michael picked him up and hugged him tight. Michael shook Vance's hand, hugged Destiny, and, when he saw Althea, walked to her, hugged her tightly, and held her for a long time. Vance cleared his throat and got their attention. Althea and Michael released each other at that moment.

Michael asked Althea, "Will you ride home with me, Althea?"

Althea said, "Yes, I will ride with you. Thanks for asking."

Antonio asked, "Dad, Mom, may I ride with Granny and Papa?"

Vance said, "Only if they say it's okay."

Althea and Michael said in unison, "Of course you can ride with us, Antonio."

Michael retrieved his bag and found the rental car, and they all left going to Althea's house.

They all arrived home in record time. Althea and Michael were getting out of the car. Michael picked Antonio up and carried him in the house and put him to bed, since he was fast asleep. Michael and Vance then returned to the car and brought in their bags.

Michael had made reservations at the hotel not far from Althea's home. Althea and Destiny went in the house and started preparing dinner.

Althea asked Michael, "Michael, you do plan to stay and have dinner with us, correct?"

Michael said, "I would love to stay for dinner."

Vance and Michael were sitting in the living room playing with Briana and waiting for dinner to be prepared.

Vance asked Michael, "Have you given any thought to our conversation, Michael?"

Michael wasn't sure which conversation he was referring to, so he asked, "Which conversation are you referring to, Vance?"

Vance said, "The conversation concerning your telling Mom how you feel about her."

Michael smiled and said, "I have been giving much thought to what you said, and maybe it's time I do express my true feelings to Althea."

Vance said, "I am glad you are taking my advice. You only live once, Michael, and life is too short not to be happy."

Destiny came out and said, "Michael and Vance, dinner is almost ready. Michael, Mama would like to speak with you in the kitchen."

Vance looked at his wife and said, "Do you know what that is about?"

Destiny smiled and said, "No, but I hope that means that they are going to stop being coy and admit that they like each other. Daddy's been dead for fifteen years now, and I think he would want Mama to be happy. I think Michael makes Mama happy."

Vance hugged his wife and said, "I think you are right, babe. They are like high school kids when they are around each other, all giddy and such."

Michael joined Althea in the kitchen per her request, and he sat at the counter waiting for Althea to join him.

Althea asked Michael, "Would you like something to drink?"

Michael said, "Yes, Althea. A soda would be fine if you have one."

Althea opened the fridge and removed two cans of cokes, and she retrieved two glasses from the cabinet. She rinsed the glasses and sat them on the table. Michael opened both cokes and poured them in each glass, handing one glass to Althea.

Althea began the conversation by saying, "Michael, I asked you to come in the kitchen because there is something I would like to share with you."

Michael held up his hand and said, "Althea, please allow me to go first. I came here today because I feel as though you and Destiny are a part of my family, as close to a family as I have. Althea, I have fallen in love with you over the years and would like to pursue a relationship with you."

Althea sat there for a moment, allowing Michael's words to sink in. She finally spoke and said, "Michael, I am so glad that we now have this elephant on the table. I was not sure how to voice my feelings, so I am glad that you said what was on my mind as well. I feel comfortable enough to share my heart with another now. Edwin has been dead for fifteen years, and I think he would approve of you."

Michael leaned across the counter and kissed Althea, and the kiss was much better than he ever imagined.

The next morning, Althea needed eggs for breakfast.

Destiny said, "Mama, I can go to the store for you if you will watch the kids for me."

Althea said, "Sure, baby, I appreciate you going to the store for me. Make sure to get some orange juice as well."

Destiny said, "Okay, Mama," got the car keys from off the bar and went to the store. Destiny was walking down the produce section when she heard someone say, "Destiny Drake, is that you?" Destiny turned to her left and saw Eric. She said, "Hello, Eric. Yes, it is me, but my name is Destiny Harmon." Eric looked confused, as if he could not comprehend the new name. Destiny explained, "I have gotten married since you saw me last. Eric, it has been almost five years since we last saw each other."

It was at that very moment when a very pregnant woman walked up and said, "Oh, honey, there you are." She was about five feet and ten inches, had skin the color of toasted almonds and long hair that she wore in twists, and appeared to be about seven months pregnant.

Destiny said, "Hello, I'm Destiny, and Eric and I were best friends when I lived here."

The girl introduced herself and said, "Hi, Destiny, I am Maurine, and I have heard so much about you. Eric and I are married, and we are expecting our first child."

Destiny said, "It's nice to meet you, Maurine. Congrats to you both on your marriage and the baby. I should be going now."

Maurine asked, "Destiny, are you married?"

Destiny turned and said, "Yes, Maurine, I am married, and Vance and I have two beautiful children. I hope to see you all while we are here. I look forward to introducing you both to my husband and children."

Destiny got the eggs and orange juice, paid for her purchases, and left the store. Destiny took the orange juice and eggs in the kitchen to Althea.

Destiny said, "Mama, guess whom I saw at the store."

Althea said, "Whom did you see?"

She told Althea, "I saw Eric and his wife, Maurine. She looked to be about seven months pregnant."

Althea said, "Yes, Eric began seeing her right after you left, and they got married about a year or so ago."

Destiny said, "I see. She appeared to be upset because Eric spoke to me in the store. I introduced myself and assured her I was happily married with two beautiful children."

Althea said, "Good, I hope that put her mind at ease."

Vance walked in the kitchen, kissing Althea on the cheek and his wife on the lips. He asked, "Is breakfast ready yet? Michael and I are starving."

Althea said, "Breakfast is almost ready; you all wash your hands and get Antonio up so he can eat too."

Vance left the kitchen and did as he was told.

Everyone came to breakfast. Althea had cooked scrambled eggs, bacon, ham, grits, hash brown, fresh strawberries and grapes, toast, coffee, and orange juice.

Althea looked across the table at Michael and said, "I guess now is as good a time as any to share the news."

Destiny and Vance looked from Althea to Michael, and they both said in unison, "What news?"

Michael smiled, and then he said, "Destiny, Vance, Althea and I talked last night, and we decided that it is time to take our friendship to the next level. As you know, Destiny, we have been friends for over seven years now, and I have loved Althea since the first time I saw her."

Vance said, "Gosh, it is about time! Destiny and I were wondering how long it was going to take the two of you to figure out that you loved each other. It is obvious to us in the way you two look at each other, how you finish each other's sentences, and the fact that you both love Destiny dearly. We are so proud of you two, and we support this relationship 100 percent."

Destiny got up from the table. She first hugged her mother and then hugged Michael. She said, "Now when I introduce you both as my mom and dad, I will be telling the truth. I love you both."

After breakfast, Destiny and Althea cleaned the kitchen and dishes, and then they sat at the kitchen table to talk.

Althea said, "Destiny, are you really happy that Michael and I decided to further our friendship?"

Destiny said, "Mama, I am truly happy. You and Michael have liked each other for a long time, but out of respect for Daddy, you chose not to act on those feelings. Mama, Daddy is gone, and it has been fifteen years since he was taken from us in the accident. He would have wanted you to be happy. I think he would have liked Michael and would approve of your sharing the rest of your life with him!"

Althea let out a sigh and said, "Baby, that means so much to me, and I am grateful for your understanding and acceptance of our decision."

The next day, the Drake and the Harmon families were in a very somber mood. It was time to say goodbye to a loved one, Marcellus, who died before his time. Destiny sat with her sister and put her arm around her to ease the pain that she knew was present. Marcellus was an only child, and that made his death harder to accept. Everyone who knew the family was at the church. The church was overflowing with people, showing their love for Marcellus as well as the family. Althea, one of the family members chosen to speak at the funeral, expressed her love for Marcellus, told of his accomplishments to include being a member of the football team in high school as well as college, and finally told of how much he was loved and would be missed by his son and the remainder of the family.

After the funeral was over, the repast was held in the fellowship hall, adjacent to the church. Althea and Destiny didn't attend the repast; instead they went to Althea's house to get away from the crowd and to have some private moments with the family. Michael was sitting with the family providing love and support to Althea. Destiny was glad that he was there to provide the support and strength that her mother needed. Althea said, "The hardest thing is for a parent to bury her child. That should not be the case. In the event that a child dies before their parents, a void is created within the family. That void is felt by everyone who knew and loved that child."

Althea was getting ready to prepare dinner, when Michael said, "Althea, you have always served others. It is now time for us to serve you."

Michael, Vance, and Destiny prepared dinner that evening; and Althea's only chore was to spend time with her beloved grandchildren. Vance made the salad; Destiny made the barbecued pork chops and mushroom gravy; and Michael made garlic mashed potatoes, creamed corn, and dinner rolls. Once everything was complete, Michael made a plate for Althea and carried it out on a serving tray. Althea thanked Michael and enjoyed her meal while watching her grandbabies enjoy their dinner.

It was Sunday and time for church. Althea and Destiny fixed breakfast and fed everyone with the exception of Michael, who agreed to meet them at church. Destiny first dressed Briana in a beautiful lavender dress with purple lace around the hem, white tights, and black Mary Jane shoes. Briana had lavender and purple barrettes in her hair. She looked totally adorable. Antonio was dressed in charcoal pants with black suspenders, a light-gray shirt, and a charcoal vest to match his pants. Vance wore a black pinstripe suit, white shirt, black and gray tie, and black wingtip shoes, looking very debonair. Destiny was a sight to behold; she wore a dark-purple fitted sheath dress, with pleats at the waist to accent her still small waistline. She wore black and purple pumps and carried a matching bag. Her jewelry was simple, gold hoop earrings and a gold necklace with a pearl attached. Last but not least, Althea wore a black suit with a cream silk blouse, gold earrings, and the diamond necklace given to her by Destiny for her birthday, with black kitten heel shoes. Michael wore a black suit with a white shirt, a string tie, and black boot-type shoes.

Just as the Drake and Harmon families were seated on their pew, Destiny observed Eric and his very pregnant wife walk into the sanctuary. Eric spotted Althea, and he came over to speak to her. Destiny used the time to introduce her husband and children to Maurine and Eric. Maurine despite her being pregnant took the time to openly admire Vance, as if her husband was not present.

Maurine finally said, "Destiny, you have a beautiful family. I can see why you were in a hurry to get home the other day." She said this while looking at Vance with lust in her eyes.

Destiny said, "Thank you, Maurine. I am rather fond of my husband."

Maurine and Eric walked away after Destiny's comment.

The announcing clerk said, "Would all the visitors please stand?" Vance and Michael were the only two who stood.

Vance said, "Good morning. It is an honor to be in the house of our Lord. I am Vance Harmon, and I am here with my wife, Destiny; our son, Antonio; and our daughter, Briana. We are visiting Mrs. Althea Drake."

It was then Michael's turn for introductions, and he said, "Good morning. I am Michael Thornton, and I am here visiting Mrs. Althea Drake and her family. I am pleased to worship with you once again."

The clerk said, "Thank you, Mr. Harmon and Mr. Thornton; we do hope that you will come and worship with us again."

After church, everyone who once knew Destiny as a young girl walked over and talked to her. They were so happy to see her and her family.

The pastor walked over and said, "Sister Destiny, it is good to see you and your family here with us today. Sister Destiny, what is it that you do again? Work I mean."

Destiny explained, "Pastor, both my husband and I are in the military. We are presently stationed in Heidelberg, Germany. We came home for my nephew's funeral."

Pastor said, "I see. We are glad to see you any time you come home, Sister Destiny." The pastor hugged Destiny, shook Vance's hand, and walked over to speak with Althea and Michael.

Vance and Michael treated Destiny and Althea to dinner after church services. Everyone enjoyed the time to relax and just "be" after all that had happened.

Althea finally asked, "When are you all returning stateside for good?"

Destiny knew the question was directed to Michael more so than to her and Vance; but she took the liberty to say, "Mama, we have only sixteen months left in Germany before we return stateside. I am not sure where we will be stationed though."

Althea said, "I see."

Michael finally spoke and said, "Althea, I have about two years left on my present assignment, and I am not sure where I will go after that. I have been serving my country for a long time. Maybe it's time I retire."

Destiny looked at Michael with confusion on her face and said, "Michael, the military is all that you have ever done. Why would you retire now?"

Michael said, "Destiny, life is too short to not be happy. Maybe it's time I reconsider my options."

Althea said, "Michael, I know you enjoy your job, and if you decide to retire, let it be because that is what *you* want. Do not do this for me. I will be here when you decide you are ready to retire."

They finished dinner, had dessert, and went over to Althea's house. Destiny asked, "Vance, can you please take me to the cemetery? I would like to go see Daddy for a while."

Destiny went to the cemetery, and she laid a single red rose on her father's grave. She removed the leaves that had fallen on his headstone, and she talked to her father. She told him about his grandchildren, Vance, her career, and how she felt. When she had said everything that she needed to say, she touched her lips with her hand, and she laid the kiss upon his headstone. Vance watched from a distance as his wife shared that moment with her father. He walked over after he witnessed his wife placing a kiss on her father's headstone; he felt that she needed his love and support at that very moment. He hugged his wife, and they walked from the cemetery arm in arm.

The next day, Vance and Destiny took the children to the museum. They visited the Snowden House, the Civil War House, and a few other historic sites that were associated with the area. The children as well as Vance enjoyed the museum, and after the tour of the museums, the kids were hungry. They had a picnic lunch in the park, and after their lunch they did some shopping. All in all, it was a very good enjoyable day for the entire family.

Vance, Destiny, and the children went to his parents' house to stay for a few days. The senior Harmons were so happy to see their son, daughter, and grandchildren. Vance and Destiny were shown to a wing on the left side of the house. The room that they would be staying in was light teal in color, with beautiful dark teal curtains. There was an antique sleigh bed against the north side of the room; a beautiful Tiffany lamp sat on a dresser that looked hand-carved from the finest wood known to man. There was a sixty-five-inch television on the south wall facing the bed, for the guest enjoyment and entertainment. The carpet was thick and fluffy under their feet, and it was beige in color. On the wall to the right of the bed was a painting of an African-American woman holding her child to her breast. Beneath the painting was an antique rocking chair that was made from bamboo, and it had an African throw draped over it. Destiny fell in love with the room. Though Vance grew up spending time in the room, he was moved by his wife's reaction to the bamboo rocking chair.

The children were placed in a room next door to their parents' room, with an adjoining door. That room was beige in color. It contained a crib that was fashioned from gnarly pine that had been smoothed to the touch; a beautiful pink blanket with butterflies embroidered around the top was lying in the crib. There was also a twin-sized bed that had been carved from the same gnarly pine and smoothed to the touch. Both pieces of furniture were expertly carved and stained. The bed was adorned with blue sheets that had cars and trucks on them with a matching comforter. There was a chest against the west wall that had the lid open, and it contained an assortment of toys for both boys and girls. The children's room was just perfect for them. Destiny was moved by the amount of time her in-laws had spent making sure that her children would be comfortable and happy. Once everyone was properly settled in, they joined the senior Harmons in the main wing of the house.

Mrs. Harmon took off from work to spend the day with her grandchildren, son, and daughter. She spent most of her day with the children, and once they were put down for a nap, she asked the housekeeper to make sure they were okay while she and Destiny spent time together. Thelma Harmon and Destiny spent the afternoon sitting on the patio, enjoying the sun and fragrance wafting off the rose garden as the wind blew.

Destiny said, "You have a beautiful home, and thank you for the care you took to ensure our family was comfortable. I especially love the rocking chair in the room that we are in."

Thelma explained, "Most of the antiques that you see in that wing are from my parents and grandparents; I just restored them so that I would have lasting memories of them."

Destiny said, "You did a beautiful job with the restoration; they are truly beautiful pieces of furniture."

Thelma said, "Thank you, Destiny, and the chair will be a gift to you from me for Briana's room."

Destiny said, "Thank you very much for such a beautiful gift" and hugged Thelma.

Vance walked out to the patio just about the time his mother and wife were hugging. He had spent the day at the florist working with his father. This was a busy time of the year, because his father was responsible for making corsages for proms, graduations, weddings, and etc., not to mention the many deliveries that were needed in the corporate center. It was Valentine's Day; and Ramon Harmon spent the entire day making deliveries in the corporate center and surrounding neighborhoods last year, and he did not get home until seven, due to the number of clients who had made orders for floral deliveries that day. Ramon often smiled when he mentioned that day, because after all the deliveries that he made, he forgot to bring flowers to his wife, Thelma. Thelma was very understanding. She hugged him when he walked in the door and had his bath run; and they enjoyed a candlelit dinner under the stars. He knew he was a lucky man.

That night, despite the beautiful surroundings, Destiny was awakened yet again by another bad dream. This time she dreamed that her husband was sick, and he was in the hospital. Each time she tried to get close to Vance, the doctors and nurses would push her from his room and lock the door. Finally, she screamed, "He is my husband, and you can't stop me from seeing him." She woke Vance up with the scream, and he shook her gently until he had her awake. Destiny was crying.

Her husband asked, "Was it another bad dream, Destiny?"

She said, "Yes, I am sorry to have woken you, Vance. That was not my intent."

Vance held her in his arms stroking her back until she calmed down. He then held her while she drifted off to sleep again.

CHAPTER 8

Distress

Destiny had suffered more pain than anyone her age would be expected to endure. She now had a loving husband, two beautiful children, and a beautiful home and life; and that should be enough for most to be happy. Destiny had truly been blessed by any standard; but despite all the blessings that she had been given, those blessings could not prevent her from being beset by dreams that haunted her each night in her sleep.

Destiny was beginning to worry that something might be wrong with her, due to these terrible dreams she kept having. She considered making an appointment to speak with the chaplain, but then she wondered would that be enough.

Vance suggested, "Destiny, why don't you talk to a psychiatrist about these dreams? Maybe they are a manifestation due to your father dying and leaving you at a very young age. It would seem that these dreams are most prevalent when things start to take a turn for the worse or when negative things happen."

Destiny said, "I will be okay; they will stop as soon as things slow down and I stop stressing over the smallest details. After all, I have the best husband in the world, and you love me very much. That makes everything better already."

Vance was not relieved by his wife's show of bravery toward her dreams, so he took the liberty to speak with the psychiatrist that he saw when he returned home from Desert Storm, after losing his best friend in the war. He called and set up an appointment with Dr. Fisher.

Vance explained, "I just wanted to talk to you about a private matter that concerns me."

Dr. Fisher explained, "Vance, I have an appointment at three o'clock, if you would like to see me then."

Vance agreed to the designated appointment.

Vance arrived at Dr. Fisher's office ten minutes early and checked in. He sat in the waiting area looking through a magazine until it was time for his appointment. At precisely three o'clock, Dr. Fisher came out and greeted Vance. David Fisher was about six feet, with athletic body that could be considered slim and tortoise shell glasses, and was probably in his mid- to late fifties, with gray hair. By most standards, he was a very handsome man. He had green eyes and a smile that always seemed to reach his eyes, welcoming everyone he met. Dr. Fisher escorted Vance back to his office.

Once they were seated, he began by saying, "Vance, it has been a while since we talked. So what brings you in today?"

Vance explained, "Dr. Fisher, I am married now, and I am not here about *my* woes, but those of my wife. You see my wife has been having dreams, or nightmares about me getting hurt. In her first dream, I was falling down the stairs, and later that day her nephew was killed. In her most recent dream, I was sick and in the hospital, and the nurses and doctors wouldn't let her see me. They locked the door to keep her away from me. She woke up screaming, *He is my husband, and you can't keep me away from him.* I am concerned and curious as to what might have triggered these dreams."

Dr. Fisher listened to everything Vance had to say, and he asked one question, "What changed in your wife's life before these dreams started?"

Vance thought about the question before he answered, and finally he said, "A series of events took place. First, she came down on orders to go to Germany when we were dating; and, second, we married three weeks before she left. Then during that same time, I came down on orders to join her. Third, she found out about Antonio, my son, whom I had before we met. Finally, eight months into our marriage, she was pregnant, and now we have a beautiful daughter too."

Dr. Fisher looked at Vance and stated, "Vance, that is a lot for any individual to accept in such a short time. I would like to speak with your wife if she is willing to see me. Please let her know about our meeting today and ask if she would be willing to see me. Vance, if your wife agrees to a meeting with me, please give me a call. I will keep an appointment open just in case."

Vance stood, shook hands with Dr. Fisher, and said, "Thank you, Dr. Fisher."

Vance returned to his parents' home and spoke with Destiny. He explained, "Destiny, I spoke with a friend of mine who was able to help me work through some tough times when I returned here on leave from Desert Storm. I watched my friend get killed in that war, and it was not easy for me to accept. His name is Dr. Fisher, a psychiatrist, and I was wondering if you would be interested in talking to him about these dreams that you keep having."

Destiny looked at her husband and said, "If you think he might be able to help me understand these dreams or why they started back all of a sudden, when it has been years since I had one, then I would be willing to give him a try."

Vance hugged Destiny and said, "I will give him a call in the morning and see when he can fit you in."

"Vance, you are coming with me to see him, right?"

He said, "Yes, but I will not sit in on the session."

She nodded and said, "Thanks, Vance, for loving me so much."

The next morning, Vance was true to his word. He called Dr. Fisher and explained that Destiny would be willing to see him whenever he had the time. Dr. Fisher checked his schedule and asked, "Can you all come in this evening at two?" Vance checked with his mother to see if she could keep the children for a couple of hours while he and Destiny had some alone time. After it was confirmed that a sitter was available, Vance then checked with Destiny and informed her of the time available.

Destiny said, "If we have a sitter for the children, I would be happy to see him today."

Vance assured her, "I checked with Mom, and she would be happy to watch Antonio and Briana for a couple of hours for us."

Vance and Destiny arrived at Dr. Fisher's practice at ten minutes to two. At precisely two, Dr. Fisher walked out into the waiting room, greeted Vance, and introduced himself to Destiny.

He said, "Good afternoon. I am Dr. David Fisher, Destiny, and it is a pleasure to meet you." He extended his hand to Destiny.

She shook it, and she then introduced herself, "Hello, Dr. Fisher, I am Destiny Harmon, and it is nice to meet you."

Dr. Fisher ushered Destiny back all the while talking to her to make sure she was comfortable. Vance remained in the waiting room as he had promised Destiny beforehand.

Dr. Fisher's office was very calming instead of clinical, the way Destiny had imagined it would be. The walls were a pale yellow. There was a comfortable couch against the north wall and a window that had a view of the ocean; and there was a photo of him and his family on a mahogany desk that sat in the center of the room. The floors were hardwood and were polished until they shone like glass. There were certificates on the wall that designated to his training, and there was an hour glass of sand that sat on an ornate stand that was carved from gnarly pine. It was the most outstanding feature in the room. Dr. Fisher sat in a chair across from Destiny.

Dr. Fisher asked Destiny, "What is your occupation?"

Destiny replied, "I am in the military."

The next question was, "Where are you from?"

Destiny answered, "I am from Arkansas."

The third question sort of caught Destiny by surprise, because she was not expecting this question, "What happened to your father?"

Destiny paused for a moment, and then she replied, "My father was killed in a car accident when I was a teenager."

Dr. Fisher asked, "What happened to him?"

Destiny replied, "He was leaving for work on a Friday evening, and he had just stopped at the stoplight two blocks from our home when a drunk driver ran the stoplight and hit him head-on killing him on impact."

Dr. Fisher asked, "How do you know this?"

Destiny replied, "I saw it in a dream the night before it happened."

Dr. Fisher asked, "Did you tell him about the dream?"

Destiny replied, "No, I was too afraid to talk about it."

Dr. Fisher asked, "Was that the first dream that you had of this nature?"

Destiny replied, "Yes, that was the first dream that I ever had; and each time from that point on in my life, when something was going to happen to someone I cared about, I would have a terrible dream before it happened."

Dr. Fisher asked, "What happened in your life just before the dreams reoccurred?"

Destiny replied, "I gave birth to our daughter, Briana, five months before the dreams started back."

Dr. Fisher asked, "How did you feel about being pregnant?"

Destiny replied, "At first I was frightened about being pregnant and had fears of how our life would change due to the pregnancy."

Dr. Fisher asked, "Did you share these fears with your husband?"

Destiny replied, "Yes, but as the months passed, I began to feel better about the pregnancy."

Dr. Fisher asked, "Destiny, what traumatic event took place in your life before you met your husband?"

Destiny sat for a moment before answering the question, and then she took a calming breath and said, "My platoon and I were attacked on a night maneuver, and my platoon sergeant and I were critically injured. Fifteen members of my platoon died that night in the attack."

Dr. Fisher asked, "How did those events make you feel?"

Destiny took a deep breath and then replied, "I was hurt, confused, scared, and angry and thought I would die on that field that night; I also wondered why this ordeal happened to us."

Dr. Fisher said, "Destiny, we can stop here if you would like, and we can continue this conversation at a later date if you would like."

Destiny said, "I am only going to be stateside for another week before my husband and I return to our duties overseas."

Dr. Fisher said, "I would like to schedule a two-hour appointment with you before you leave returning overseas."

Destiny nodded and said, "I will make the appointment on my way out."

Destiny made the appointment as directed, and she and Vance were returning to her in-laws to check on the children. Destiny informed Vance of her scheduled appointment, and they agreed she should return for the session. For the first time in three years, Destiny thought about the incident and how it changed her life. *She wondered if all that she had endured happened as a precursor to bring her to this point in her life. She was a firm believer that all things happen for a reason. Though an individual may not know the reason at the time things are happening, they are all part of God's plan for that individual, and in time, they are manifested to the individual.* Destiny closed her eyes, laid her head back, and cleared her mind of the incident and any worries that were associated with that fateful night. She concluded *it was God's will.*

That evening, Vance and Destiny returned to find Thelma and the kids having a picnic on the patio.

Antonio was the first to see his parents, and he said, "Granny, my mom and dad are home."

Thelma turned around and said, "Yes, just when I thought I would have you two for a little while longer."

Vance picked up Antonio and gave him a hug, and Destiny leaned over and kissed him while he was in Vance's arms, causing the child to squeal with delight. Then they did the same with Briana. She giggled as well. Thelma watched the exchange and a smile spread across her face.

She said, "Destiny, you are a great mom."

Destiny looked at Thelma and said, "Thank you. It's easy when I have great kids like these two."

Thelma informed Destiny and Vance, "Dinner will be ready in about two hours; if you all are hungry, I could make you a sandwich."

Both Destiny and Vance said, "We are fine. Just let us know when you are tired of the munchkins, and we will come and get them."

Thelma said, "Go for a drive or something and be back in time for dinner. Let me enjoy the babies!"

They laughed and did just that. Vance showed Destiny all of his old hangouts that he visited when he lived at home. Destiny was in awe of some of the dives her husband would hang out at, but the ride down "memory lane" was time well spent.

Destiny and Vance arrived in time to freshen up for dinner and spend time with their favorite "little people." Destiny played with both Antonio and Briana in their room with toys from the toy box. Vance sat and admired how his wife chose toys carefully and began to play with them in order for their children to want to play with those toys.

Vance tried to join in on the fun, but Antonio said, "Dad, you are not doing it right. Let Mom do it. She knows how it works."

Vance smiled and said, "Okay, 'little man,' I will let you guys play with your mommy."

Vance pretended to be hurt by Antonio's comment, and Antonio came and gave his dad a big hug. The four of them had fun until they were called for dinner.

Everyone sat down to dinner, and Ramon said grace. Thelma was a very good cook; and she had made fried rice, chicken kabobs, chicken nuggets (for the kids), salad, and corn on the cob and made pudding, a dessert she knew Antonio and Briana would enjoy. After dinner, Vance and Destiny cleaned the kitchen and washed the dishes. Once they were finished with that chore, they told Briana and Antonio to give Granny and Grandpa a kiss. It was bath time. Destiny gave each child a bath, allowing them to play with their favorite rubber duck while taking a bath. Once she finished bathing one, Vance would dry the child, apply lotion, and put on pajamas for bedtime. Finally when both children were in bed and fast asleep, Destiny and Vance informed his parents, "We are going for a walk. Would you please check on the kids for us?" Thelma was overjoyed to do so. They left and walked around the neighborhood holding hands as they walked. Vance pulled Destiny into an alcove and kissed her passionately, and after that kiss, they decided it was time to go home.

They walked back the way they had come, holding hands and happy just to have some time to their selves.

When they arrived back at the house, Thelma and Ramon had turned in for the night, and Vance and Destiny checked on the children and then readied themselves for bed. That night Vance made love to Destiny like his life depended upon it for his survival. Once their lovemaking was over, Vance placed his arm around Destiny and pulled her close. Destiny slept peacefully through the night, with no nightmares.

The next morning, Destiny prepared breakfast for her family, since Thelma went back to work. After breakfast, she and Vance packed their suitcases for their return trip to Althea's home. They readied the children and drove to the florist to say goodbye to Thelma and Ramon. Destiny thanked them both for having her and the family over, and she in turn invited them to come and visit in Germany. Destiny and Vance left going back to Althea's house.

That evening at about one thirty, Vance, Destiny, and the kids arrived back at Althea's house. Colonel Thornton drove up as they were getting out of the car, and he helped Vance with their luggage. Michael picked up Antonio and hugged him, tickling his ear, and he tickled Briana's ear as well. Both children giggled with delight.

Antonio said, "Hi, Papa, I missed you. We were at Grandma and Grandpa's house."

Michael said, "I missed you all too. It was lonesome without you guys." Michael carried Antonio in the house and told him, "I have a surprise for you and Briana."

Michael and Antonio walked back to his car, and they came back in with two stuffed animals. Antonio let his sister choose first. Briana chose the monkey, and Antonio took the elephant. They each hugged their papa and said, "Thank you!"

That evening Destiny helped Althea prepare dinner. They made fried chicken, rice with cream gravy, peas and carrots, salad, sweet tea, and cornbread. Michael had never tasted Althea's fried chicken, so from the first bite he took, he was totally in love with the taste of the chicken. It was spicy, yet delicious at the same time. He said, "Althea, if you continue to make fried chicken like this, I will be glad to retire from the Army, just so you can feed me this chicken." Everyone laughed, and Althea blushed at Michael's comment.

Vance, Destiny, Althea, Michael, and the children were sitting in the living room when all of a sudden, Michael began to sit up in the recliner, grabbed his chest, and began to sweat profusely. Althea asked, "Michael, are you alright?" Michael did not answer. Destiny picked up the phone and dialed 911. Destiny said, "We need an ambulance at 2718 Carver Street. I think my father is having a heart attack." Within ten minutes or less, the ambulance was there. The paramedics came in and ushered Michael out on a gurney, taking him to St. Michael's Hospital. Althea rode in the ambulance with Michael, holding his hand and praying that he would be fine all the way to the hospital.

Michael was rushed into the hospital, placed in a room, and connected to an electrocardiogram (EKG); and several tests were performed, and then he was given something for the pain. Althea and Destiny sat waiting in the waiting room, hoping for good news. Finally, Dr. Martin came out and spoke with Althea and Destiny.

He said, "Mr. Thornton has suffered a mild heart attack, but we were able to repair the damages, and he is going to be fine."

Althea asked, "Can we see him now?"

Dr. Martin said, "Only for a short time, and then he has to rest."

Destiny said, "Mama, you go in see him and let him know I am here if he feels up to seeing me."

Althea nodded and left with tears in her eyes. Althea entered Michael's room and went and sat by his bed. She looked at the man she loved and placed a kiss upon his brow. She said, "Michael, I love you so much, and you have got to get well so that we can get married. Destiny is out in the waiting room, and I will send her in." Althea kissed Michael again before leaving his room, and she walked back to the waiting room.

Althea told Destiny, "I need you to go and pack me some clothes. I am not leaving him here alone!" Destiny hugged Althea and left the hospital to go pack Althea a bag. Destiny arrived at the house and found Vance waiting in the living room. Destiny ran to her husband and laid her head on his shoulder and cried.

When all her tears were spent, she said, "Michael had a mild heart attack. The doctors made repairs, and he should be fine. Mama is going to stay with him at the hospital until he is released."

Vance said, "I will go down to the hotel and pack up his things and bring them over here. I will also contact his unit and let them know what has happened to Michael."

Destiny nodded her head and hugged and kissed the children and her husband before going back to the hospital.

Destiny arrived at the hospital with the bag, and Althea met her in the waiting room.

Althea said, "Thank you, baby, for doing this for me; and I will call you all if there are any changes in Michael."

Destiny kissed Althea and said, "I think I want to go talk to Michael and let him know that *we* need him to get better."

Althea said, "Okay, baby."

Destiny went back to Michael's room; she sat by his bed and took his hand. Destiny said, "Michael, you are like a father to me. I love you, and I need you to get well. Antonio and Briana need their papa too." Michael's eyes fluttered open, and Destiny rang for the nurse. The nurse came into the room and checked Michael's vital signs.

The nurse said, "Mr. Thornton, how do you feel?"

Michael said, "I feel better now that my daughter is here. I heard every word you said; and I am going to get better for you, Althea, and my grandbabies."

Destiny rose and kissed Michael on the forehead, and she went and got Althea.

The next morning, Destiny called her unit and requested additional leave due to a family emergency. Her commander granted her four more weeks of leave. Vance called and got his leave extended four additional weeks as well. Vance and Destiny took care of the paperwork concerning Michael's leave, and she took the documentation and had his doctor sign the necessary paperwork. Once all documents were complete, Destiny faxed them back to his unit. Michael was placed on emergency leave for an indefinite time, so that he could recover from his surgery.

Exactly eight days after his surgery, Michael was released from the hospital. Destiny had readied the guest room for him at Althea's house. Vance went and picked him and Althea up from the hospital.

That evening after dinner, Michael proposed to Althea. He said, "Althea, will you do me the honors of becoming my wife?"

Althea kissed Michael on the cheek and said, "Yes, I would be honored to be your wife."

Since Michael had just gotten out the hospital, the proposal was celebrated with apple cider until Michael was able to drink alcohol again. Michael asked, "Vance, would you please go to my car, look in the glove compartment, and bring me the 'red velvet box' that is sitting in the left corner?" Vance did as he was asked and brought back the box. Inside was a one-carat diamond, princess-cut ring that Michael placed upon Althea's left ring finger. Althea hugged Michael and kissed him. She was crying *tears of joy.*

Three days later, Destiny and Vance returned to Dr. Fisher's office for her appointment. At precisely one o'clock, Dr. Fisher came out and greeted Vance and Destiny. He led Destiny back to his office.

Dr. Fisher said, "Destiny, with your permission, I would like to hypnotize you to see if you are able to remember any further details from your childhood that might have led to your dreams."

Destiny explained, "Dr. Fisher, I do understand that you are trying to get to the source of my problems, but I will not concede to be hypnotized."

Dr. Fisher said, "What if I were to allow Vance to sit in on this session? Would you then agree to being hypnotized?"

Destiny replied, "I will concede to this treatment on one condition: You bring my husband in here, and you agree to bring me out if things go wrong."

Dr. Fisher said, "I agree to your terms, Destiny." He went and asked Vance to come in the office so that he could be present during the time Dr. Fisher hypnotized Destiny.

Dr. Fisher pulled a beautiful silver orb from his coat pocket. He explained to Destiny and Vance that he would speak to her in a calm voice while slowly swinging the orb for her to watch. He would ask her to count backward from twenty to one, and then they should be ready to start the questions. By the time Destiny reached number "five," she was in a trancelike state, and she said, "Please forgive me. I am so sorry. I had no idea that my not telling you about the dream would result in your getting hurt. Please don't go. Why did you have to leave me? You told me I was your baby girl and that you would always love me. I tried to be a good girl for both you and Mom, but why did you have to go and leave me alone? I don't understand. Did I do something wrong? Daddy, please answer me! No, I *will not* stop asking questions. It was *me* whom you left, yet you said you loved me. You were there for my brothers and sister, but you left me. I needed you to be there for me. You missed my birthdays, my high school graduation, my college graduation. You even missed the birth of your grandchildren! Okay, go! I will be okay. I have learned to depend on myself, and I have learned to take care of myself! I will always love you, and I am sorry for keeping the dream a secret. Daddy, I miss you so much!" Destiny was crying throughout her conversation with her father. At one point, her tears were so heart-wrenching Dr. Fisher was ready to end the hypnosis, but Vance stopped him. Vance knew his wife had to experience the agony of meeting and having this conversation with her father, if she were ever going to get better.

Finally after all of Destiny's tears were spent, Dr. Fisher brought her out of the trancelike state. He then asked, "Destiny, how do you feel?"

Destiny said, "I feel like I travelled back in time and met with my father. Dad wasn't angry with me for not telling him about the dream; he told me it was God's will and I needed to stop blaming myself for his death."

Dr. Fisher asked, "Destiny, are you satisfied with the answers you received from your father?"

Destiny said, "Yes, I am. I am now at ease with his death!"

Dr. Fisher said, "I think now that you have the answers that you were seeking, your dreams will stop."

Destiny said, "Dr. Fisher, thank you for allowing me to have that moment with my father. It meant a great deal to me."

Dr. Fisher said, "You are welcome, and I knew it would."

He shook both Destiny and Vance's hands, reminding them he was just a phone call away if they needed him.

Destiny and Vance rode back to Althea's house in silence. Both were deep in thought of what they had learned that day. Destiny was glad that she finally had the chance to say the things that she wanted to say to her father, but never had the chance until today. She was now at ease with his death, her life, and all things that had bothered her. She even saw the incident that occurred that night on maneuver in a different light than she had before.

They arrived at Althea's home and found Michael sitting up playing with the children.

He asked, "Well, how did things go, Destiny?"

Destiny asked, "Vance, will you please take the children in their room to play?" Vance did as his wife had asked, and she then explained her appointment to both Althea and Michael in detail. She said, "Dr. Fisher hypnotized me, and I went back in time and talked to Dad. I thought Dad blamed me for his death, but he assured me it was not my fault."

Michael asked, "Honey, why would you think that?"

Destiny replied, "Michael, the night before Dad died, I had a dream in which I saw the entire accident take place. I was too afraid to say anything to him or Mom about my dream. The next day, a Friday to be exact, he was killed just as I had dreamed."

Althea got up and hugged her daughter with tears in her eyes and said, "Destiny, it was God's will. God had called your father home, and it was time for him to go. It had nothing to do with you. I just wish you would have trusted me enough to share that dream with me. I am sorry you carried that burden in your heart all this time. Your father loved you just as he did your siblings, and I love you all equally."

Destiny wiped away the tears that had fallen from her eyes onto her face, and she hugged her mother tightly. Destiny thanked her mother for being there and loving her unconditionally, and she also thanked Michael for being the father that she no longer had. It was a very touching moment, one that truly showed the love that had been borne from such a tragedy.

Two weeks later, Michael stood before God, Pastor Crowley, and the church congregation and professed his love to Althea and made her Mrs. Michael Thornton. That was one of the happiest days of Althea's life. Althea truly loved her husband, and it had taken fifteen years for her to get past his death and share her heart with another. She knew Michael was her soul mate, and she would spend the rest of her life loving that man. Althea said, "I am truly blessed. Most people only get one opportunity to love someone special, but God has seen fit to give me a second chance at love, and for that I am grateful!" Everyone in the church stood and clapped for the new couple, for they knew that Althea and Michael's love was ordained by the grace of God.

Exactly ten days later, Vance, Destiny, and the children left going back to Germany. Althea and Michael were enjoying their new life as husband and wife.

Michael offered to buy Althea a new house, but Althea declined saying, "I will accept and move out of this house only if it makes you uncomfortable being here. I have memories in this house. All my children were raised here, and now I want to be able to leave and share some of those memories with Antonio and Briana."

Michael smiled and said, "Althea, I will live wherever you are. I don't feel uncomfortable being here, because I have you."

Althea hugged her husband and said, "Michael, thank you for understanding, but most importantly, thank you for loving me."

The following day, Althea and Michael received a call from Destiny and Vance alerting them that they had arrived home safely.

Vance told Michael, "I hope you don't mind, but I took the liberty to speak with your commander, and he would like for you to fax him a copy of your marriage certificate, so that he can complete your benefits for Althea. He will be faxing you the necessary paperwork to complete so that he can get the process started."

Michael said, "Thank you so much, Vance. I will give him a call when I hang up from you."

Michael called his commander, and his commander said these words, "Colonel Thornton, congratulations on your nuptials, and I am glad to hear you are doing better. Whenever you are ready to return, your post will be available and waiting."

Michael said, "Sir, thank you for your kindness. I spent some time thinking while I was laid up in the hospital, and I came to the conclusion that God has seen fit to bless me with a second chance at life; and I think I am going to take advantage of *his* blessing. Sir, I will be returning soon to retire from the service and spend time with my wife and newly acquired family."

Michael's commander said, "Colonel Thornton, I do understand. I am sure if I were in your position, I would do the same."

Four months from the date of Michael's conversation with his commander, he and Althea boarded a plane to Germany. They arrived at Michael's unit, spoke with his commander, and then packed up Michael's quarters in Germany. Michael signed the required documents, to include his retirement paperwork; took his eight months of leave that he had acquired, ensuring that he exchanged four months of that leave for pay purposes; and took the other four months of leave to show his wife around Germany. Michael retired with twenty-eight years of service to his country; he earned several commendations to include a bronze star. He said goodbye to all his friends, and then he left going to visit his son and daughter in Heidelberg, Germany. Althea was so proud of her husband and his dedication to his county, unit, and family. She knew she had been blessed with a great man and husband!

Michael and Althea took a month and toured Europe. Michael was so happy to introduce his wife to one of the most diverse countries in the world and allow her to experience a different culture. One of their first stops was Venice, Italy. Michael and Althea went on the *Prosecco Wine Tasting Tour* and tasted the various wines that were made and sold in Venice their first day there. Day 2 in Venice consisted of a walking tour of St. Mark's Square as well as the *Basilica*, which is a church that is known for its art and history. The walls appear to be made from twenty-four-carat gold; and angels, archangels, and other heavenly beings are depicted in drawings that cover the walls from the ceiling to the floor. The *Basilica* overlooks St. Marks's Square on the edge of the Grand Canal and is joined to the Doge's Palace. In the ninth century, merchants smuggled St. Mark's relics out of Egypt and brought them to Venice. The scene is depicted in the oldest known exterior mosaic in the world located above the cathedral's front doors (1260–1270). Althea was amazed at the beauty of the architecture as well as the furniture and art design.

Just before the sun began to set, Michael persuaded Althea to go with him on a gondola ride. The ride was very romantic; they sailed past beautiful villas, historic palazzos, and cathedrals on their gondola ride. They were serenaded by a local musician who entertained them with Venetian ballads while they toured the Grand Canal for thirty-five minutes transporting Althea and Michael to another place mentally, while they were plied with Venetian wine from one of the finest wineries. From there, they were sailed various smaller canals and were then transported to *Hostaria Ai Coristi*, one of the finest restaurants in the country. There they enjoyed a four-course meal of the finest cuisine ever served, and Althea enjoyed the evening. Althea was sure things could not get any better than these first two days spent in this beautiful country, but her husband assured her the best was yet to come.

On their third and final day in Venice, Michael and Althea travelled by water taxi to Murano Island. They went on the *Glass Blowing Tour*, where Althea was afforded the opportunity to try on *Cinderella*'s glass slipper. Althea and Michael also had an opportunity to try their hand at glass blowing during the demonstration process, and Michael proved to be pretty good at glass blowing. They walked through the showrooms of the glass factory and purchased some pieces for Althea and Destiny. They spent the remainder of the evening shopping on Murano Island.

Althea and Michael returned to their hotel, exhausted and happy. Althea thanked Michael for allowing her to enjoy three lovely days in such a romantic country. That night, for the first time, they consummated their marriage. Michael fell asleep knowing that he was one of the luckiest men in the world to have found Althea and love this late in his life.

The second place that Althea and Michael visited was Paris, France. Althea had dreamed of going to Paris ever since she was a young girl, but now she was touring this romantic city with her husband. From the moment they arrived in Paris, it was evident that Althea was smitten with Paris. From the excitement in her step to the smile that encompassed her face, there was no doubt that Althea was right where she wanted to be. Michael asked one of the locals, "Would you please take a picture of me and my wife in front of the Eiffel Tower?" The man conceded, and he took a picture of Althea and Michael arm in arm in front of the Eiffel Tower. Michael said "Thank you" to the local who took the picture, and he continued the tour with his arm locked around his wife.

Michael wanted to visit the *Catacombs of Paris*, former mines from the eighteenth century that were transformed into a subterranean labyrinth graveyard. These catacombs house the bodies of many souls that perished in the French Revolution. Althea forbade him from visiting the catacombs because she thought it too strenuous following his surgery. After all, there are eighty-three steps that lead down and out of these catacombs.

Althea and Michael did tour *Sainte-Chapelle*, or the "Holy Chapel." King Louis IX built this beautiful chapel that had marvelous stained-glass windows and floating chandeliers, for the Crown of Thorns to be housed, before they were moved to Notre Dame. Tourist from around the world travel to see the beauty of this sacred place, and Althea was so moved by the beauty of this chapel that she cried as they were walking around. Michael was really touched by the appreciation that his wife had for the relics that they had seen thus far.

Althea said, "Michael, thank you for sharing the beauty of this country with me."

Michael kissed his wife and said, "Althea, this is one of the many things I hope to share with you during our time together."

They walked hand in hand and chose a nice bistro to have lunch. They had a typical French lunch which consisted of a mixed salad, a bowl of soup, meat or fish with rice, pasta, and/or vegetables. They had the salad, onion soup which was flavorful and spicy, fish that was so flaky it appeared to melt in one's mouth, and rice with green beans. For dessert, Althea had an apple tart. The tart was so buttery and delectable. Althea savored every bite she took.

Finally, their tour was over; and they stopped to visit Destiny, Vance, and the children. Destiny noticed that her mother was glowing, and she was so happy for Althea and Michael.

Destiny said, "Michael and Mama, why don't you two spend a couple of weeks here with us before returning stateside?"

Althea said, "Baby, we will only be able to spend a week with you all. Michael has to return for his checkup."

Destiny said, "We understand, and we are happy to have you all for as long as you can stay."

That week flew by. Althea and Michael babysat the children while Destiny and Vance worked and spoiled them tremendously. Briana was turning into a "papa's girl." She enjoyed spending time with her papa and granny.

Destiny had been home six weeks now, and she had not had any more dreams since she had been to visit Dr. Fisher. Destiny sent Dr. Fisher a "thank you" note along with a beautiful stein and a box of German chocolate.

Dr. Fisher received the stein, and he called Destiny and said, "Mrs. Harmon, thank you very much. I received my chocolates and the stein today. My wife ate my chocolates and handed me the stein."

Destiny said, "Dr. Fisher, you are welcome. I have not had any dreams since returning to Germany. Please tell your wife to expect more chocolates in a week or so."

They laughed and signed off.

Two weeks later, Destiny went to check their mail; and there was a letter addressed to her husband from Hawaii. Destiny went home and placed the letter on the kitchen counter so that Vance would see it when he came home. Two hours later, Vance came home. He kissed Destiny and hugged both Antonio and Briana.

Destiny said, "Vance, there is a letter on the kitchen counter from Hawaii."

Vance walked to the counter, picked up the letter, opened it, and read it. Vance turned to Destiny and said, "Destiny, this letter is about Antonio's biological mother. She was found dead from a drug overdose in her apartment."

Destiny walked to her husband, held him close, and said, "I am truly sorry that this has happened. I understand if you would like to take Antonio to the funeral."

Vance held his wife and said, "We are not going. Antonio's mother is holding me right now, and that is the end of things."

Destiny was so happy to hear her husband say those words, because she loved Antonio just as much as she did Briana; and to her, he was her son.

The following weekend, they celebrated Briana's first birthday. Destiny could not believe it had been a year since she had given birth to her darling daughter. Briana was walking, talking, and being a complete terror around the house; but her parents wouldn't have wanted it any other way. She was beginning to gain her own personality now; and when her brother would do something to irritate her, she would stop, put her hands on her little hips, stamp her foot, and scream, "Stop, 'Tonio!" Vance thought it was adorable, but Destiny would punish her daughter for that type of behavior. She was sure she had the makings of a brat, and that was unacceptable as far as Destiny was concerned.

The following day, Althea and Michael called and said, "How is Granny and Papa's birthday girl doing?" They also informed Destiny that the presents for both Briana and Antonio were in the mail and they should be there in a couple of days.

Destiny said, "Antonio and Briana, your granny and papa are on the phone. Come and say hello."

The children came running into the room, and they were both talking to Althea and Michael at the same time.

Michael was so happy to hear their voices, and he said, "Papa loves you both very much, and Granny and I will be there for Christmas."

This was enough to have Briana and Antonio saying, "Yay, we love you, Granny and Papa. Hurry and come home!"

Althea also told Destiny, "Michael received a clean bill of health from his doctor, and he no longer requires a special regimen. We will continue to exercise and eat healthy. I changed my cooking habits after his heart attack, and he only gets fried chicken once every three months or so."

Destiny said, "I am so proud of you all, and I love you both. We are counting down the days until you get here."

LEGEND

Military Ranks

When hiring or working with a Veteran, it may be helpful for you, as an employer or supervisor, to better understand what his or her military experience or title means. You may look at the resume and see titles or abbreviations that have little meaning to civilians. This handout provides information about the difference between types of rank (enlisted vs. officer) and the hierarchy of the ranks.

Each rank is listed from lowest to highest in the chain of command for each branch.

Military Rank

E	Enlisted	An enlisted member is one who has joined the military or "enlisted." A minimum of a high school diploma is required.
NCO	Noncommissioned Officer	An NCO is an enlisted member who has risen through the ranks through promotion. NCOs serve as the link between enlisted personnel and commissioned officers. They hold responsibility for training troops to execute missions. Training for NCOs includes leadership, management, specific skills, and combat training.

W	Warrant Officer	A warrant officer is a highly trained specialist. One must be an enlisted member with several years of experience, be recommended by his or her commander, and pass a selection board to become a warrant officer.
O	Commissioned Officer	A commissioned officer's primary function is to provide management and leadership in his or her area of responsibility. Requires a bachelor's degree and later, as one progresses through the ranks, a master's degree for promotions. Specific commissioning programs exist (e.g., military academies, Reserve Officer Training Corps [ROTC]).

Army Ranks

Pay Grade	Title	Abbreviation
E-1	Private	PVT
E-2	Private 2	PV2
E-3	Private First Class	PFC
E-4	Specialist	SPC
E-4	Corporal	CPL
E-5	Sergeant	SGT
E-6	Staff Sergeant	SSG
E-7	Sergeant First Class	SFC
E-8	Master Sergeant	MSG
E-8	First Sergeant	1SG
E-9	Sergeant Major	SGM
E-9	Command Sergeant Major	CSM

E-9 Special	Sergeant Major of the Army	SMA
W-1	Warrant Officer	WO1
W-2	Chief Warrant Officer 2	CW2
W-3	Chief Warrant Officer 3	CW3
W-4	Chief Warrant Officer 4	CW4
W-5	Chief Warrant Officer 5	CW5
O-1	Second Lieutenant	2LT
O-2	First Lieutenant	1LT
O-3	Captain	CPT
O-4	Major	MAJ
O-5	Lieutenant Colonel	LTC
O-6	Colonel	COL
O-7	Brigadier General	BG
O-8	Major General	MG
O-9	Lieutenant General	LTG
O-10	General	GEN
Special	General of the Army	GA

Air Force Ranks

Pay Grade	Title	Abbreviation
E-1	Airman Basic	AB
E-2	Airman	Amn
E-3	Airman First Class	A1C
E-4	Senior Airman or Sergeant	SrA
E-5	Staff Sergeant	SSgt
E-6	Technical Sergeant	TSgt
E-7	Master Sergeant	MSgt
E-8	Senior Master Sergeant	SMSgt
E-8	Senior Master Sergeant	SMSgt
E-9	Chief Master Sergeant	CMSgt

E-9	Command Chief Master Sergeant	CCM
E-9 Special	Chief Master Sergeant of the Air Force	CMSAF
O-1	Second Lieutenant	2d Lt
O-2	First Lieutenant	1st Lt
O-3	Captain	Capt
O-4	Major	Maj
O-5	Lieutenant Colonel	Lt Col
O-6	Colonel	Col
O-7	Brigadier General	Brig Gen
O-8	Major General	Maj Gen
O-9	Lieutenant General	Lt Gen
O-10	General Air Force Chief of Staff	Gen
Special	General of the Air Force	GOAF

Navy/Coast Guard Rates

Pay Grade	Title	Abbreviation
E-1	Seaman Recruit	SR
E-2	Seaman Apprentice	SA
E-3	Seaman	SN
E-4	Petty Officer 3rd Class	PO3
E-5	Petty Officer 2nd Class	PO2
E-6	Petty Officer 1st Class	PO1
E-7	Chief Petty Officer	CPO
E-8	Senior Chief Petty Officer	SCPO
E-9	Master Chief Petty Officer	MCPO
E-9	Command Master Chief Petty Officer	MCPOC
E-9	Fleet Master Chief Petty Officer	FLTCM
E-9	Force Master Chief Petty Officer	FORCM

E-9 Special	Master Chief Petty Officer of the Coast Guard	MPCOCG
E-9 Special	Master Chief Petty Officer of the Navy	MCPON
W-1	Warrant Officer	WO1
W-2	Chief Warrant Officer 2	CWO2
W-3	Chief Warrant Officer 3	CWO3
W-4	Chief Warrant Officer 4	CWO4
W-5	Chief Warrant Officer 5	CWO5
O-1	Ensign	ENS
O-2	Lieutenant, Junior Grade	LTJG
O-3	Lieutenant	LT
O-4	Lieutenant Commander	LCDR
O-5	Commander	CDR
O-6	Captain	CAPT
O-7	Rear Admiral (lower half)	RDML
O-8	Rear Admiral (upper half)	RADM
O-9	Vice Admiral	VADM
O-10	Admiral Chief of Naval Operations /Commandant of the Coast Guard	ADM
O-10 Special	Fleet Admiral	FADM

Marine Corps Ranks

Pay Grade	Title	Abbreviation
E-1	Private	Pvt
E-2	Private First Class	PFC
E-3	Lance Corporal	LCpl
E-4	Corporal	Cpl
E-5	Sergeant	Sgt

E-6	Staff Sergeant	SSgt
E-7	Gunnery Sergeant	GySgt
E-8	Master Sergeant	MSgt
E-8	First Sergeant	1stSgt
E-9	Master Gunnery Sergeant	MGySgt
E-9	Sergeant Major	SgtMaj
E-9 Special	Sergeant Major of the Marine Corps	SgtMajMarCor
W-1	Warrant Officer 1	WO1
W-2	Chief Warrant Officer 2	CW2
W-3	Chief Warrant Officer 3	CW3
W-4	Chief Warrant Officer 4	CW4
W-5	Chief Warrant Officer 5	CW5
O-1	Second Lieutenant	2ndLt
O-2	First Lieutenant	1stLt
O-3	Captain	Capt
O-4	Major	Maj
O-5	Lieutenant Colonel	LtCol
O-6	Colonel	Col
O-7	Brigadier General	BGen
O-8	Major General	MajGen
O-9	Lieutenant General	LtGen
O-10	General	Gen

ABOUT THE AUTHOR

D.J. Parrish resides in Lacey, Washington. She lives with her teen-age son. She is a veteran of the US Army and worked in education as well as criminal justice before becoming a writer. When she is not writing, she enjoys creating crossword puzzles, reading, cooking, bowling, sports, video games, and spending time with her family and friends.

CPSIA information can be obtained
at www.ICGtesting.com
Printed in the USA
LVHW052308200319
611369LV00001B/87/P